P9-CMX-446

"Do you think Tucker's still being teased?"

"I wouldn't be surprised." Meg folded her arms across her chest. "I better go up and check on him. He can't miss any more school."

"Do you want me to go with you? I might be able to talk to him," Luke offered.

"I'm not trying to be rude, but I'd rather you didn't speak with Tucker. In fact, I'd rather you stay away from him as much as you can during your stay at the inn. I don't want him to get pulled into the world of cowboys or get too attached to you, since you won't be staying permanently. I hope you understand."

Luke bit his tongue and nodded.

Introducing Tucker to mutton busting could help the boy gain confidence. Before his uncle took him to his first competition, Luke had been withdrawn from his family and friends. As much as he could understand the reasons behind Meg's reservations about Tucker getting involved in the rodeo world, he didn't agree with her.

He'd have to figure out a way to change her mind.

Weekdays, **Jill Weatherholt** works for the City of Charlotte. On the weekend, she writes contemporary stories about love, faith and forgiveness. Raised in the suburbs of Washington, DC, she now resides in North Carolina. She holds a degree in psychology from George Mason University and a paralegal studies certification from Duke University. She shares her life with her real-life hero and number one supporter. Jill loves connecting with readers at jillweatherholt.com.

Books by Jill Weatherholt

Love Inspired

Second Chance Romance
A Father for Bella
A Mother for His Twins
A Home for Her Daughter
A Dream of Family
Searching for Home

Visit the Author Profile page at LoveInspired.com.

Searching
for Home

Jill Weatherholt

LOVE INSPIRED
INSPIRATIONAL ROMANCE

If you purchased this book without a cover you should be aware that this book is stolen property. It was reported as "unsold and destroyed" to the publisher, and neither the author nor the publisher has received any payment for this "stripped book."

LOVE INSPIRED®
INSPIRATIONAL ROMANCE

Recycling programs for this product may not exist in your area.

ISBN-13: 978-1-335-75901-6

Searching for Home

Copyright © 2021 by Jill Weatherholt

All rights reserved. No part of this book may be used or reproduced in any manner whatsoever without written permission except in the case of brief quotations embodied in critical articles and reviews.

This is a work of fiction. Names, characters, places and incidents are either the product of the author's imagination or are used fictitiously. Any resemblance to actual persons, living or dead, businesses, companies, events or locales is entirely coincidental.

This edition published by arrangement with Harlequin Books S.A.

For questions and comments about the quality of this book, please contact us at CustomerService@Harlequin.com.

Love Inspired
22 Adelaide St. West, 40th Floor
Toronto, Ontario M5H 4E3, Canada
www.LoveInspired.com

Printed in U.S.A.

We love him, because he first loved us.
—*1 John* 4:19

To my beautiful mother.
Thank you for always loving me for who I am.

Chapter One

Appliances should never be allowed to break on a Monday morning.

Meg Brennan unplugged the toaster oven, launching sparks and puffs of smoke into the kitchen of the Trout Run Bed and Breakfast.

"Should I call the fire department, Aunt Meg?" Six-year-old Tia Petrino sprung from the cedar bench that lined one side of the table.

Meg scooped the blackened pastries from the oven and tossed them into the sink. "That won't be necessary."

Tilly placed her elbows on the table and her hands under her chin. "Oh, man. Those were the last three doughnuts." Her lower lip rolled.

Meg pulled in a slow and steadying breath. *One day at a time.* That's how she'd handled things since her sister and brother-in-law abandoned their triplets and the B&B last year. She glanced toward Tucker sitting at the end of the table. The poor child hadn't smiled since his parents left. First his father and then his mother. "Tuck, we don't have enough time for your favorite chocolate chip pancakes, but would you like some cereal instead?"

"I don't care." He shrugged his shoulders and opened the book in front of him.

Meg considered his words. Sadly, Tucker didn't seem to care about much of anything.

The front doorbell chimed. Meg glanced at her watch. Time was like an icy road this morning. The kids had to catch the school bus soon.

"I'll get it!" Tilly bolted toward the front of the house. Her yellow tennis shoes with pink laces screeched against the hardwood floor.

The child had never met a stranger. Meg tossed the red dish towel on the granite countertop and moved toward the hall. The front lock clicked, and the hinge in need of tightening on the screen door squeaked.

"Wow! Are you a real-life cowboy? Like the ones we see on TV?" Tilly's question echoed down the hall.

"I was interested in a room, but I noticed the tarp on one side of the house. Are you open?"

Meg's ears burned at the familiar deep voice.

Luke.

Seventeen years had passed. The pain was still raw.

Standing in the foyer, his muscular frame was larger in person than on television. Not that she watched him on purpose. Sometimes she'd sneak a quick peek when a guest or the children had the sports channel on in the gathering room.

"He's a professional bull rider, Tilly." Meg stepped toward the door. The grandfather clock, in the family for years, sat in the corner and ticked off the seconds.

A smile parted his lips. "Meg—I wasn't expecting to see you here." Luke took off his cowboy hat, revealing close-cut dark hair.

Her breath slowed when she recalled how soft his hair had felt the first time they'd kissed during junior prom. "I don't know why not. This is where I lived when you left me to chase your bull riding dream. What was it—the day after you turned eighteen?"

His steel-blue eyes scanned the room. "I remember the house, but not the bed-and-breakfast."

Tia skipped into the room. Her chestnut curls skimmed her shoulders.

"Look, Tia! We've never had a cowboy stay here."

Inching closer to her sister, Tia stole a glance at the guest.

Tilly tipped her chin up. "They really pay you to ride bulls? That's so cool!"

From what Meg recalled, he got paid a lot of money. The last time she saw the standings, Luke was ranked as one of the top earners. Just like her father—until an injury stole his career and eventually his life.

"I used to think so," Luke whispered.

If Meg hadn't had her eyes parked on his full, rosy lips, she would have missed what he said. So, cowboy life wasn't all it was cracked up to be. But you couldn't deny life as a bull rider had transformed his boyish good looks into a muscular and chiseled man.

Luke moved his gaze to Meg. His cheeks flushed. "Do you have any rooms available?"

Meg's mouth dropped open before she turned her attention to Tilly and Tia. "Girls, go eat your cereal. And make sure Tuck's eating, too."

"Tuck won't listen to us." Tilly spun on her heel and ran toward the kitchen. Tia followed her sister.

Meg worried about Tucker, but right now she had an even bigger problem standing in the middle of her foyer. A six-foot, five-inch problem. "You can't be serious about the room—are you?" *Please say no.*

"I am if you're open for business."

He was serious. "Yes. I've got one room, the hummingbird suite, available this week. The other two are closed for repair." She chewed her lower lip. "Still, I don't think it's a good idea for you to stay here."

Luke rubbed the back of his neck. "I get it. Your husband probably wouldn't like it too much."

Husband. "What makes you think that I'm married?"

"The kids." He placed his luggage on the floor.

Meg's throat tightened. No. He needed to pick up his bag and go back to Colorado or wherever he came from. "The girls are my nieces. Gina's kids."

He nodded. "Right, Gina. So—there's no husband?" He flashed a smile that used to make her weak in the knees. But not anymore.

Meg raised her left hand and wiggled her fingers in his face. "You tell me."

Luke laughed. "You've still got that spunk I always loved."

A long pause filled the room until she felt like she was drowning in memories. "I'm not the same girl you left behind, Luke." She squared her shoulders. "I think it would be best if you stay at the Black Bear Resort. Are you familiar with it?"

"I read about it online, but it's not what I'm looking for."

"Given your lifestyle, I'd say it's perfect for you. This place would probably be too quiet." The thought of passing on a paying guest caused her stomach to sour, but having Luke Beckett under her roof was worth a couple of late fees on the already mountainous stack of outstanding bills.

Luke's expression turned solemn. "I don't want to go into details, but I've come to Whispering Slopes to get away from the spotlight. I need to stay somewhere that's quiet, and where I won't be recognized."

Was he in some sort of trouble? She couldn't take any chances with the triplets.

Luke half laughed. "Don't worry, I haven't committed any crime." He paused and ran a hand across his unshaven chin. "I just need a break—that's all."

For a second, a twinge of sympathy filled Meg's heart. She nodded and swallowed hard. "I'll admit, I can relate to that."

"Thank you. I promise to stay out of your way in the coming weeks."

Weeks. She'd never agree to that. One or two nights maybe…but weeks? "Exactly how long do you plan to stay?"

"Six weeks—maybe longer." His eyes bored into her.

Meg wrapped her arms tight around her slim waist. "I'm not sure that's going to work. Besides, can you take off that much time?"

"Let's just say it's a forced vacation. Look, I know I'm the last person you want as a guest, but I'll pay anything. You said some of the rooms are closed for repairs. I'll cover the loss you're taking—please. I'm begging you."

Meg considered his plea. Was there more to this than an extended vacation? What kind of secret was he keeping? "I can't let you pay for rooms you won't be occupying."

"So, you're in charge of this place?"

Meg brushed the pads of her fingers across her forehead. "I took it over early last year."

"Do you and Gina own it together? That's pretty cool considering you both grew up here."

It would have been cool, if Gina's husband hadn't up

and left his family, leaving Gina depressed and feeling ill-equipped to provide the emotional and financial stability her children needed. Gina had trusted her older sister to do a better job raising the triplets. "No. I own and operate it alone. Gina isn't in the picture." Why on earth had Gina married so young? And why had Meg ever promised her sister she'd keep the B&B open for the children to maintain a sense of normalcy?

Luke scratched his head. Giggles sounded from the kitchen. "Where is she?"

"Your guess is as good as mine." If Luke planned to stay here for any length of time, he'd find out soon enough. "Gina and her husband abandoned their kids and signed over their rights to me. I haven't heard from either since." Babies having babies. They hadn't been prepared to start a family.

"Oh, Meggie."

Meg's heart squeezed at the sound of the nickname he'd given her their freshman year of high school. A lifetime ago. "I don't need your pity or your charity. You will pay the cost of one room or no deal."

"Whatever you say. May I ask what's wrong with the other rooms?"

"We had a big storm a few weeks ago. The roof suffered significant damage. The insurance company covered the replacement cost, but there was substantial interior damage that wasn't covered. Gina and Greg, my brother-in-law, had the most basic coverage on the property. Neither had a good head for business. They weren't qualified to open a B&B. There's a second mortgage on the property and not enough money to cover all the bills." Her chest tightened.

"You might not remember the clubhouse I built as a teen, but I'm still pretty handy with a hammer and paintbrush. Maybe while I'm here, you'll let me take a look. I can save you some money." He stepped in a little closer. "Of course, you haven't given me a green light on the room."

The phone wasn't exactly ringing off the hook for reservations. As uncomfortable as it might be with Luke as a guest, Meg had to admit, six weeks of guaranteed cash flow would relieve some of the stress.

"I can pay for six weeks upfront—if that helps."

It was as if he'd read her mind. She couldn't do that... could she? No. That might encourage him to stay even longer. Maybe paying for a week at a time would keep his trip shorter than he planned. "That's not necessary." Meg pulled her cell phone from the back pocket of her skinny jeans to check the time. Her pulse quickened. "I've got to get the kids ready for school. Their bus will be here any minute. If you want to get settled into your room, it's upstairs—the first door on the left. We can get you signed in later."

"Sounds good. Thanks again. I know I'm not your first choice for a guest, but I'll lie low and stay out of your way. In fact, once I put my bag away, I think I'll go for a long hike in the woods. It's a beautiful day."

Maybe it wouldn't be so bad. If she could get a few repairs done at no cost, it would certainly help with her cash-flow issues. Just because they'd be under the same roof, it didn't mean they'd have to see each other every second of the day. Perhaps she could get away with only seeing him at mealtimes. "If you head down toward the larger of the two barns, my brother-in-law made a nice trail. It circles the back of the property. It's about three miles."

"That's exactly what I need. Thanks for the suggestion." He picked up his luggage and ascended the stairs. At the landing, he paused and turned around, his expression solemn. "I'm sorry for leaving you." He hesitated.

Was he waiting for her to accept his apology? The hair on the back of her neck tingled. "Let's leave the past where it belongs."

With that, Luke turned and headed to his room.

Meg's mind drifted to the day she discovered Luke had left. He'd written a three-page letter, but she'd never read past the first two sentences. Those six words had turned her world upside down. *I'm sorry. I have to go.* At the time, she didn't need to know anything more. Or maybe she didn't want to know. He was gone and there was nothing he could say that would change that fact. She'd stuffed the unread letter into her diary, where it remained.

Out front, the school bus's brakes hissed and the horn honked, pulling Meg back into the moment. "Kids! Grab your backpacks. The bus is out front."

The girls giggled while they skipped down the hall toward the front door.

"'Bye, Aunt Meg." First Tia and then Tilly hugged Meg. "Love you," they both chirped.

"Have a good day, sweeties. Where's Tuck?"

The girls shrugged and rushed out the door.

"Tucker—come on, honey. You're going to miss the bus."

Meg waited until Tucker appeared. The child walked toward her with his head down. Once at the door he stopped and turned. "My stomach hurts."

Here we go again. The same routine each day. Tucker complained of a tummy ache and she'd reassure him it would go away once he got to school. "You'll be okay, sweetie." Meg bent down and kissed his cheek. "Have a good day. I'll be here when you get home."

He trudged out the door and toward the bus. Meg's heart ached for the child. Could the stomachaches be real? Was he afraid to leave the house because he feared when he got home, she wouldn't be there—just like his parents? *Gina, what were you thinking? Why didn't you try and seek professional help after Greg left?*

Following a thorough cleaning in the kitchen, Meg headed upstairs to put some fresh linens on Luke's bed. Miss Mattie had the morning off. On a normal day, she would take care of cleaning the rooms and getting guests settled, but today was anything but normal. Luke's arrival was proof of that.

Earlier, Meg had heard the front door open and close, so the coast was clear. Luke had left for his hike. She'd slip in and take care of his room before he returned. If she timed it right, perhaps she could make it until lunchtime without seeing him again. Never in her wildest dreams had she imagined Luke would be a guest at her B&B. Of course, she'd never thought she'd be raising triplets, either. Life was certainly unpredictable.

A short time later, Meg tucked the last corner of the top sheet underneath the mattress. With a few fluffs of the yellow throw pillows, she arranged them against the carved mahogany headboard of the four-poster bed. She stepped out into the hall to grab some clean towels from the linen closet for her only guest.

Inside Luke's bathroom, she placed pima cotton bath towels, along with a washcloth, on top of the double-sink vanity. Turning to head out, her eyes caught sight of a prescription bottle next to Luke's leather shaving kit. *It's none of your business.* Yet something pulled her closer. Without touching the container, she leaned in. Pain pills. Her mind flooded with memories of her father. Was this why Luke had been placed on a mandatory vacation? Was he addicted to pain medication like her father?

Later that afternoon, Luke ventured outside to the front porch of the B&B. He settled into the red cedar swing with a copy of the latest Western novel penned by his favorite author. Since he was a young boy, he'd enjoyed the genre. Funny, the life he lived didn't seem quite as exciting as it did between the pages of the books he devoured.

The hike earlier in the day had helped to clear his mind. Spring in the Shenandoah Valley had always been his favorite time of the year. When he was young, he'd head to the meadow to pick wildflowers for his mother. She'd put the bouquet into a crystal vase then place it on their kitchen table. In her eyes, it was the one thing he could do right—until he started to win trophies at competitions. It was then his parents began to pay more attention to him. He'd finally found a reason for them to love him, so he had to keep winning.

Luke's cell phone pinged an incoming text. He removed the device from the back pocket of his denim jeans and tapped the screen. The bright sunshine cast a glare across the screen. Luke squinted to read the message from his agent, Reed Cushman. The note contained the date, time and address of the doctor's appointment he'd scheduled for Luke. After he'd told Reed he had no intention of taking the pain medication the doctor had prescribed, his agent said he would need to see a physical therapist as soon as possible.

After a quick reply to thank him, Luke pocketed the phone. He probably should have mentioned his neck injury to Meg, but he'd come home to Whispering Slopes with hopes of recovering outside the spotlight. Reed was trying his best to keep Luke's absence from competition low-key to prevent any loss of national sponsors. Plus, Luke knew if Meg learned of his injury, she wouldn't allow him to help with the repairs on the two bedrooms. And that's exactly what he intended to do.

Through the open screen door, he could hear pots and pans clattering inside the house. Since returning from his hike, he'd made a point to stay clear of Meg, who appeared busy in the kitchen. Just because they shared a history and had once talked about spending their lives with one another didn't mean he could get under her feet. She had a business to run.

Besides, after what he'd done, she probably wouldn't even consider him a friend. Once upon a time, Meg had been the most important person in his life, but he'd blown it by taking the easy way out and leaving town without talking to her face-to-face.

But as an insecure teenage boy, he'd struggled with expressing himself. Pouring his heart out onto the blank piece of paper had seemed like the best way to make sure Meg knew she was only part of the reason he had to leave town. He wanted to become a successful bull rider first. Then he would be worthy of asking for her hand in marriage. And unlike what his father had said, he'd be able to provide for Meg and their future children.

The last thing he'd wanted was for Meg to think the only reason he'd left for Colorado was to chase a big dream that didn't leave room for her. She had a starring role in his dream. But she must have agreed with his parents since she'd never reached out to him after reading his letter. Now he had no one except his fans. But like his parents, they only loved him conditionally—when he was winning.

Luke looked up at the sound of an engine rumbling. The bright yellow bus with black lettering came to a stop at the end of the driveway. Within seconds the door opened, and Meg's nieces hopped down the steps. Each toted a sparkly, pink backpack. Their curly chestnut hair glistened in the sunlight. One of the girls pointed to the porch, leaned in and whispered to the other. Seconds later they both took off running toward the house. Gravel crunched underneath their tennis shoes.

Next, the boy exited the bus. Tucker. That's what Luke remembered Meg calling him. With his head down, kicking a rock, he made his way up the driveway. A dark blue windbreaker dragged on the ground behind him. The child appeared oblivious to his surroundings.

"You're still here." One of the two girls stepped forward. The resemblance made it nearly impossible to tell them apart. "I'm Tilly." She stretched out her hand and flashed a smile, revealing a missing front tooth. If the other had all her front teeth, he would be good.

"Yes, I'm still here. It's nice to meet you, Tilly. I'm Luke Beckett." He took her hand, and she gave him a big shake while her sister stayed quiet. Tilly was obviously the outgoing one of the two. "And what's your sister's name?"

"I'm Tia." She moved a little closer but kept her hands stiff against her sides. A slight smile parted her lips, exposing all her front teeth.

"It's nice to meet you, Tia."

Tilly examined the book resting in Luke's lap and giggled. "That's funny you like to read about cowboys."

He'd never thought so. Maybe it was a bit unusual, but it was a way for him to escape the pressure of competing and the need to be the best. "What kind of books do you like to read?"

Tilly flopped down on the swing. "I like mysteries." Her legs kicked back and forth. "It's fun to try and figure things out."

"Not me." Tia jumped up on the other side of Luke. "I like books with animals."

He smiled. Maybe she wasn't so shy after all. "What's your favorite animal, Tia?" Luke's eyes focused on Tucker. He stood on the other side of the porch next to the flower boxes that were exploding with red geraniums.

"Monkeys!" Tilly exclaimed.

"Til...Cowboy Luke asked me, not you." Tia folded her arms across her chest.

Luke stifled a laugh at his new name. "Monkeys are cool. What about you, Tia?"

The girl tapped a finger on her lower lip as if she was answering the hardest question on a test at school. "Well, I really have two. I like goats, but my favorite are sheep. My mommy used to say Tucker reminded her of a sheep."

Luke glanced in the boy's direction before turning back to Tia. "Did she say why?"

"Because he's so meek," Tilly interjected.

The screen door squeaked, and Tucker sprinted toward the open entrance.

While holding the door, Meg watched the child bolt past her and straight up the stairs. She faced his sisters. "Girls...what did you do to make Tuck so upset?"

"Tilly told Cowboy Luke Tucker is meek, like a sheep." Tia jumped off the swing, picked up her backpack, and ran inside.

Meg frowned. "What have I told you about teasing your brother, Tilly?"

"It wasn't my fault—honest." Tilly looked at Luke before she climbed off the swing and stopped in front of Meg. "It was Cowboy Luke's fault." And with that, she zipped inside the house.

Meg pulled the door closed behind her and walked toward the swing. "Care to explain, Cowboy Luke?"

Like a protective mama bear, Meg waited for an answer. Luke cleared his throat. "We were talking about animals. Tia mentioned Gina used to say Tucker reminded her of a sheep. I thought maybe it was because he's cute or something." He paused and turned for a second. "I should have known. I'm sorry."

"He's a sensitive little boy. He's had a hard time since his parents left, more so than the girls." Meg pivoted on her heel and went indoors.

Luke's stomach turned over. Of course he should have known. Wasn't that what his mother used to compare him to? A fearful and directionless sheep. His older brothers were perfect in his mother's eyes, but never him. His siblings had been planned, but not Luke. He'd been an unwanted surprise to his parents. It was only when he began to win trophies at bull riding competitions that his parents paid more attention to him. Winning made Luke feel wanted and loved, like his brothers. Luke recalled the look on Tucker's face before he ran inside. He knew how the boy felt. Perhaps the rooms in the B&B weren't the only thing in need of repair.

Chapter Two

Tuesday morning, Meg pulled the sheer curtain away from the front window. Buttery sunlight streamed into the gathering room as she watched the triplets board the bus. Another hectic start to her day. Like a broken clock, she was behind the moment her feet hit the floor. The girls had fought over a sweater and poor little Tucker had complained about his stomach—again.

"Mr. Beckett only wants coffee this morning. He said he's heading out for the day, so no breakfast or lunch." Miss Mattie scurried down the steps, and both women headed to the kitchen.

Meg could never keep the B&B running if it weren't for Mattie Henderson. At seventy years old, she had the energy of a teenager. Miss Mattie had moved to Whispering Slopes at the same time Meg was looking for help last year. God's timing couldn't have been more perfect. "That should make for an easier day, especially since I'm seeing a new patient later this morning."

"I'm happy to hear that, dear. You know, if you'd like to expand your hours at the office, I would be more than happy to cover for you here. I could keep an eye on the children. I know how much it means to you to help others get well again." Miss Mattie removed a serving tray from the cabinet and placed it on the counter.

Shortly after Meg had given up her practice working as a physical therapist in Richmond, she'd returned to Whispering Slopes and rented office space in town. She'd wanted to help Gina with the children. After Gina's husband had left, her sister had become depressed and suffered a nervous breakdown. Meg had tried to get her the proper help, but no social worker or psychologist could save her sister. In the end, Gina had signed over her rights to the children. She loved them, but she wasn't capable of raising them.

Meg's promise to keep the B&B open and raise the children brought her joy, but treating patients was a passion that wouldn't loosen its grip. She'd never had the opportunity to heal her father, so as long as there were enough hours in the day, she'd make herself available to the residents of Whispering Slopes.

"I appreciate that. I might need to take you up on your offer. My appointments are backed up since my landlord had the office closed the past two weeks to do some painting. I have two other sessions scheduled for tomorrow."

"I've got you covered." Miss Mattie poured the coffee and placed the cup on the tray next to the plate of chocolate-and-almond biscotti. "I better get this up to our guest so he can start his day."

"Thanks." Meg was relieved she wasn't the one serving Luke this morning. Yet being under the same roof for possibly six weeks, she would have to get used to having him around. She couldn't avoid him forever.

Meg stepped toward the coffeepot and poured the remnants into her travel mug, then headed outside to her car. On the drive into town, her mind wandered.

Luke didn't want breakfast. That seemed odd. When they were younger, Luke had always had an enormous appetite. Then she thought of her father. He'd always preferred pills over the meals his wife cooked. He'd claimed he wasn't hungry. Had the pills she'd seen yesterday in Luke's bathroom stolen his appetite, too? As much as she wanted to confront him about the medication, it wasn't a good idea. He'd think she'd been snooping even though that hadn't been her intent.

Once at her office, Meg parked and exited the vehicle with her thoughts remaining on Luke. She would have to keep a close eye on him. As long as he was under her roof, she would not allow him to end up like her father.

"Good morning, Doc Brennan."

As she stood on the sidewalk in front of her office, the morning sun warmed her back. Meg turned the key in the doorknob and pivoted to the sound of Ben Chadwick's voice. "Good morning to you, Mayor. How is your knee feeling?" Last winter he'd taken a hard spill on an icy sidewalk. Once the swelling had subsided and he was able to walk without significant pain, Meg had worked with him to rebuild strength and flexibility in his thigh and leg muscles to restore a full range of motion to his knee.

"Thanks to you, it's feeling pretty good. A little stiff in the mornings." He lifted his foot away from the cement and gave it a little shake. "Probably old age." He laughed.

"You could have some arthritis settling in." She stepped inside the building and placed her coffee on the front desk. "Did you want to schedule a session?"

"I was hoping to. I'm relieved to see you're open again. Elsie Buser will be happy. I know she's been having some trouble with her elbow."

Meg had to admit, as difficult as it had been to leave her practice in Richmond, she loved working in a small town. She pulled out the black leather chair and sat down in front of the computer. With a few keystrokes, she was in the scheduling program.

"I don't know how you do it all," the mayor said. "Running the B&B, caring for the triplets and taking care of us. I think it's time you have someone to take care of you."

"That's kind of you to say, but I'm doing fine on my own. I prefer it this way." Depending on others only led to heartache. "Let's see…I have two sessions scheduled for tomorrow morning. I can put you down for the afternoon before the kids get home from school. Does twelve-thirty work for you?"

The mayor removed his phone from the inside pocket of his powder-blue seersucker jacket and swiped the screen. "I've got a chamber of commerce meeting at ten o'clock, so that's perfect." He tapped the appointment into his calendar before returning the device to his pocket.

Meg's eyes scanned today's schedule. Reed Cushman. The name didn't sound familiar, but the appointment had been scheduled through her website. Perhaps he was from a nearby town. With a little time before her first appointment, she hoped to update a few patient records.

Mayor Chadwick lingered in front of the desk. "Rumor has it the big-time rodeo star has returned home to Whispering Slopes."

Luke had wanted to keep his presence in town quiet. Could it be because of the pills? Regardless, Meg had given Luke her word that she wouldn't tell anyone he was here. "And who would that be?"

"Luke Beckett, of course. Elsie claimed she saw him driving through town yesterday morning in an expensive-looking oversize pickup truck. You know her, she doesn't miss a thing. Bless her heart." He laughed. "I thought maybe Luke would pay you a visit since you two were so close."

Meg's stomach squeezed. That was then.

A ringtone chimed, and Meg relaxed. Saved by the bell.

The mayor checked his phone. "Excuse me, but I've been expecting this call. I'll see you tomorrow. Thank you for working me into your calendar."

She nodded and watched him head out the door. Luke had done more than visit her, but it wasn't her place to spread the news. Unless Luke hunkered down at the B&B like a hermit, it was only a matter of time before the town would be buzzing about his return. What would they think about the fact he chose to stay at the Trout Run rather than the Black Bear Resort? She couldn't worry about that. Gossip came with the territory of small-town living.

Thirty minutes later, Meg had updated four patient accounts when the front bell rang. She saved her document and pushed away from the cherry desk located in her office behind the reception area. She entered the common area, and her feet skidded to a stop. Heat prickled the back of her neck. "Luke?"

The muscular frame spun around, and his eyes popped. "Meggie?" He moved closer and focused on the sign displaying her name and logo, hanging prominently behind the front desk. "You're a doctor?"

"Yes, I'm a physical therapist." Her shoulders straightened.

Luke's brow crinkled. "But you always wanted to be a teacher."

"I suppose there are a lot of things you thought you knew about me. Now, if you'll excuse me, I have a new patient coming any minute. The last thing I want is for him to walk into the middle of our trip down memory lane."

Luke laughed.

"What's so funny?" Meg crossed her arms.

"I'm your new patient."

Meg slipped into the chair behind the computer. Her fingers fumbled over the keyboard. She couldn't type fast enough, but then she relaxed. "Trust me, your name isn't on my schedule."

"I know you have to keep patients' names confidential, but your appointment wouldn't happen to be with someone named Reed Cushman, would it?"

Meg dropped her hands against the desk. Her heart rate accelerated. "How did you know?"

"That's my agent's name. He scheduled the appointment for me."

Talk about a small world. But then again, she was the only physical therapist in town since Dr. Meyer had retired six months ago. Heat flared in her face. *Put your personal feelings aside. Be professional. Luke is just another patient.* That's what her head told her, but her heart was speaking a different language.

Luke held his breath while he waited for Meg to speak. The hum of the computer's fan filled the room.

"I'm not sure I understand. Why would your agent set up an appointment for you using his name?"

Luke knew his agent was trying to keep his presence in Whispering Slopes quiet. Reed didn't want to jeopardize the lucrative sponsorship deals he'd been negotiating. "I suppose he's trying to safeguard my privacy. My injury hasn't been officially made public. I have some endorsements he's trying to protect."

Meg stood and rounded the desk. Her eyes connected with his. "You were hurt? Why didn't you say anything? Are you going to be okay?"

The compassion in her voice touched him, but where had that empathy been after she'd read his letter? Luke understood her reasons for disliking bull riding. He'd seen Meg's father deal with consistent injuries. "Yes. I was bucked during an event earlier in the month." After being hooked and hooved so many times, Luke thought little about the injury, but he was growing older, and injuries took longer to heal. "The doctor said I'll be fine. It's only a strained trapezius."

"Only?" Her lips pursed. "That can be serious. You can't mess around with that type of injury. The last thing you want is for the muscle to rupture."

"I understand. And that's why I'm seeking treatment." But there was no way it would be with her. It had been a painful blow when she failed to reach out to him after reading his letter. Days had turned into months and after the first year it had become clear, Meg had never truly loved him. No, this would never work—they had too much history. He'd have to find another doctor in the area.

Her eyes narrowed. "What about the pills?"

"What pills?" As soon as he asked, he remembered the medication he'd removed from his shaving kit while settling into his room. At that moment, he'd been in a lot of discomfort. For a second, he had considered taking one for some relief. In the end, he knew he would be better off working through the pain himself. He wouldn't take any chances when it came to becoming dependent.

Meg's cheeks reddened. "I was putting fresh towels in your bathroom. I saw the bottle on the vanity."

Luke nodded.

"I wasn't snooping." She rubbed her right hand up and down her left arm.

"That never crossed my mind. I know how you feel about pain medication, Meggie. I remember what was going on with your family when I left for Colorado."

Meg leaned against the desk and touched her brow. "You don't know the half of it."

He knew Meg. She wouldn't have brought it up unless it had been wearing on her mind. "Do you want to talk about it?"

"After you left Whispering Slopes, my father's injury had him in and out of drug rehabilitation centers throughout Virginia. During my second year in college, my mother gave up. She filed for divorce and moved out. I couldn't blame her. After she left, his addiction got worse. I came home from school during the holidays and pleaded with him to get help. I encouraged him to give physical therapy a try, but he refused. I went back to school, changed my major and ignored his phone calls asking for money." She brushed her eye with the back of her hand. Her face paled. "I should have tried harder to get him into rehab."

Luke moved closer, filling the space beside her. Their shoulders touched. "I'm sorry I wasn't there for you." He'd left her at a time when she needed him most. A fact he couldn't deny. But he had needed her, too. Writing the letter had been more painful than his countless falls from bucking bulls.

Meg flinched, moved behind the desk, and slipped

into the chair. "I can't talk about this any more right now."

Luke remembered how close Meg had been with her father. When she was a little girl, she'd beg him to take her along when he traveled the rodeo circuit. "Yeah, I better get out of your hair." He started toward the front door.

"Wait!" She jumped from her seat. "What about your appointment?"

Was she serious? "I think I'll just give it time and see what happens. Remember, I have a high pain tolerance."

"But you can't do that," Meg commanded. "You'll just end up taking the medication. That stuff only masks the pain. It won't treat the injury."

"I promise, I won't take any pills." He'd seen some of his friends get hooked. There was no way he'd allow that to happen.

"Without the proper treatment, you could end up with irreversible damage. If you don't ride, you don't get paid. I remember."

Luke considered Meg's comment. "Things are different from when your father competed. Endorsements and ad campaigns can be lucrative." But it wasn't money that he needed—he needed to win. If he wasn't winning, he was worthless. Even his parents thought so. And given Meg's silence after he'd left town, she must have concurred. Bull riding wasn't your average desk job. It came with risks, and he accepted them. "I'll get it checked. I'm sure there are plenty of doctors in neighboring cities."

"What about protecting your privacy? I thought that was important to you?"

True. It was the reason he'd chosen to recuperate in Whispering Slopes and not a large city. "I'll talk to my agent. We'll figure something out."

The telephone on the reception desk rang, but Meg didn't move to answer. Her eyes remained fixated on him. "Please, Luke. Let me help you."

Her plea told him there was something more than a doctor wanting to make a patient well again. "Can I ask you something?"

Meg nodded.

"What happened to your father?" Her eyes turned vacant at his question. His heart pounded.

"He passed away."

"I'm so sorry, Meg."

She sucked in a deep breath. "Bull riding—what he loved more than his family—took his life."

Strange. After he left Whispering Slopes, Luke remembered reading an article about her father's official retirement. "But I read he'd retired."

"That's true, but his career-ending injury drove him to abuse pills and alcohol. In the end, that's how he died."

The computer chimed, and Meg turned to the screen. "It's the report from your doctor. I guess your agent had it forwarded."

No doubt. Reed always covered his bases.

Meg looked away from the email. "Let me help you. I promise I'll do everything in my power to maintain your privacy." She paused and scanned the room. "We could do your treatments at the B&B, so people won't see you coming into the office. I'm sure you remember how word gets around in this town. Mrs. Buser is already telling people she thought she saw you."

Luke smiled at the memory of the elderly woman. If you wanted the latest town news, ask Mrs. Buser. "I guess some things never change."

"If you go to a bigger city like Harrisonburg or Charlottesville, you'll take the risk of being surrounded by fans with their phones. You know how social media is these days. Once something is put out there, it goes viral."

Meg would have made a good attorney—her argument was valid. Two years ago, after he'd taken a spill and suffered a concussion during an event in Texas, he'd been rushed to a hospital in Dallas. After he'd been inundated by staff and patients wanting his autograph or to snap a selfie, his doctor had agreed he'd get more rest at home. With this recent injury, he didn't want to jeopardize losing any of his sponsors.

"Plus, think of all the windshield time. Neither city is exactly a stone's throw from Whispering Slopes. Driving too much could slow the healing process, with all the head movements."

"Okay, okay!" Luke raised his arms over his shoulders, causing shooting pain down his neck. "I should have known better than to go up against the captain of our high school debate team."

Meg smiled. "I'm sorry to be so pushy, but I really want to make sure you get the proper care."

Meg hadn't changed a bit. It was in her nature to want to help him, despite their history. As much as he doubted it was a good idea for her to treat his injury, he had to agree. Going outside Whispering Slopes could create a media circus, and that was something he wanted to avoid. Living under the same roof was one thing, but having the only woman he'd ever loved help him recover was risky, especially given her feelings toward professional bull riders. He would have to maintain his focus: get better, leave town and go back to winning—the one thing that filled the gaping void and loneliness that had plagued him since childhood. "I know you do, and I appreciate your concern. I'll agree to give it a try, but under one condition."

Meg nodded firmly. "Which is?"

"I'll take care of the repairs to the B&B so you can reopen the two rooms."

"What makes you think I need your help?"

"Come on. The fact that you're allowing me to stay in your only available room is a pretty good sign that you need the money. Plus, you mentioned Gina and her husband had left a lot of unpaid bills. But most importantly, you're providing for the triplets on your own. I know it can't be easy. You want to help me—so let me help you."

Meg chewed on her lower lip. Something she'd done since she was a child. She looked adorable.

"Okay, but you have to make a promise." A line appeared between her brows. "I don't want you to do any further damage to your neck."

He saluted. "Yes, ma'am. I promise. The slightest twinge and the hammer will go back inside the toolbox."

Meg laughed.

He used to love to hear her laughter. "I always believed you'd make a great teacher, but maybe you've truly found your calling as a physical therapist, Meggie. You love to help people."

"Life doesn't always turn out the way we plan. There's been a lot of twists and turns that have led me to where I am today. I gave up my dream of teaching to study kinesiology. It's what I'm meant to do." She spoke with confidence.

What if life had turned out as they'd planned? If Luke had stayed in Whispering Slopes and they'd gone off to college together, would they be married now with a family of their own? Had his decision to prove to his parents he was worth loving created a new path for Meg? Or had her lack of response to his letter confirmed what he'd feared—that she'd never really loved him?

Meg's cell phone rang. She picked it up and looked at the screen. Her eyes widened. "Excuse me. I need to answer this."

"Of course." Luke turned to give her some privacy. He scanned the wall that housed her degrees and awards.

Just moments later, Meg's chair rolled across the floor and slammed into the wall as she ran toward the back office. *What in the world?* He turned toward the commotion.

"What's wrong?"

Meg hustled past him, her oversize purse swinging from her shoulder. "That was Tucker's teacher. I have to get to the school. He's been in a fight." She shot out the door into the bright sunlight. Her keys hit the sidewalk.

Concern took hold. "You can't drive, Meg. Look at your hands shaking." He snatched the keys from the ground. "Where's your car? I'll drive you."

Chapter Three

"You didn't have to drive me." Meg squeezed her fists tight to settle the shakes. This was Tucker's third fight in the past two months. Did first graders get suspended from school?

"I know I didn't have to, but I wanted to. You're too upset to be behind the wheel." Luke navigated Meg's SUV along the steep mountain road. "Did the teacher say what the fight was about?"

"No, but it's always the same." Meg gazed out the window in hopes the picturesque mountain view would calm her nerves.

"So, these fights aren't something new?"

"According to Principal Capello, before the triplets were abandoned, they were model students. Tilly and Tia are still doing well in school, but Tucker—I don't know. Tilly told me he thinks Gina and Greg left because he wasn't good enough. But he won't talk to me about it. Whenever I bring up his parents, he shuts down. Tucker's teacher mentioned he gets teased by a few of the boys in class. She spoke with the children, told them it was wrong, but they persisted."

"Poor guy. Kids can be cruel."

Meg turned and studied Luke's profile. He was still the most handsome man she'd ever known. But he wasn't always so well-built and strong. She remembered Luke being small for his age. Then he turned sixteen and had a major growth spurt. Every girl in school took notice. Luke only had eyes for her, though, until bull riding became more important. Bull riders—the rock stars of rodeo. That's what her mother always said. It was for the best that Luke had left her. After what she experienced with her father, she could never go down that road again. "Didn't the Baxter boys bully you when we were in grade school?"

Luke nodded. "They sure did. I spent a lot of time in the principal's office. That's another reason I wanted to come along. I might be able to talk to Tucker to see what's going on."

"I don't know. He can be shy around people he doesn't know." The last thing Meg wanted was to get Tucker more upset. She'd worked hard the past year to try and gain his trust.

"I understand. I won't push him. Did you say Principal Capello? Is that Nick?"

"It is. Can you believe it?" The three had attended school together until Nick's family left town, but he'd returned years later with his own children.

Luke shook his head and laughed. "I really can't. He might have spent more time in the principal's office than I ever did."

"Turn here." Meg pointed toward the building that housed Whispering Slopes K-12.

Luke chuckled. "I know I've been gone for a while, but do you really think I've forgotten how to get to our school? I have some great memories of this place." He hit the turn signal and guided the vehicle into the first empty spot before placing the car in Park.

Meg's eyes scanned the familiar grounds. The night of the junior prom flashed through her mind. First the kiss they'd shared on the dance floor. At that moment, Meg's world had changed forever. After, she and Luke had come outside into the courtyard, where they sat on a bench holding hands and dreaming of their future. Under a dark velvet sky, brimming with brilliant, twinkling stars, Luke had revealed his heart. He loved her. Recalling his confession caused a shiver to travel through her. But that was then, and it hadn't been enough. She couldn't hang on to the past. Tucker needed her now. She unfastened her seat belt and pushed open the car door. "Let's go see what happened."

Inside the school, Meg and Luke headed toward the principal's office. The familiar aromas of grilled cheese and tater tots drifted through the hallway.

"Boy, I'm having a major flashback." Luke's boots clicked against the tile floor.

"Only one?" Meg teased.

Luke nudged his shoulder against hers. "Funny. Okay—maybe a couple."

"I think Principal Jacobson might have known you better than his own kids." Meg turned right down a long hallway lined with colorful artwork created by the students.

"Some things never change." Luke slowed in front of a large collage containing handprints of various sizes. "Do you remember doing this?" He pointed to the hodgepodge of colors.

"I think I had paint on my hands for a week after that project." Meg stepped next to Luke and noticed him massaging the back of his neck. "Are you okay?"

He dropped his hand to his side. "Yeah. I'm fine." Luke tilted his head to one side and then to the other before they resumed their walk toward the office.

Cowboys—they'd never admit they were in pain. "I'm sorry about your appointment. Once I read your doctor's report, we can reschedule for later today, if you'd like. I can have Miss Mattie watch the children." It was important to get Luke started on a proper treatment regime as soon as possible. If he wasn't taught the proper exercises to strengthen the muscles that supported the spine and shoulder blades, going back into competition so soon could result in further injury. Exactly what her father had chosen not to do. Instead, he'd turned to pills and alcohol to dull the pain. A deadly combination.

"You might have your hands full with Tucker. Let's play it by ear."

Meg stepped inside the principal's office and spotted Tucker. Her heart sank. He sat slumped with his head down in a straight-back wooden chair against the wall. A strand of curly hair partially covered his brown eyes. He picked at his thumb, avoiding eye contact with everyone in the room.

"Hello, Meg." Nick Capello rose to his feet and offered his hand. "Thank you for coming." He turned to Luke and smiled wide. "I didn't know you were in town. It's great to see you again, buddy." The two men shook hands.

"It's good to see you, too. I'll be here for a while, but I wanted to keep a low profile. I was hesitant about coming to the school, but Meg was so upset, I didn't want her to drive."

"Keeping a low profile will be hard, especially if Mrs. Buser hears you're in town." Nick laughed. "Seriously, congratulations on all your success. I'm a big fan." Nick turned to the door. "Mrs. Cooper. Good timing. They just got here."

Mrs. Cooper, a small woman in her late sixties, stepped inside the office. "Hello, everyone."

Meg observed the older woman. Her eyes lasered in on Luke, and then her face flushed like a teenager's. She placed both hands to her cheeks. "Oh, my. You're Luke Beckett. I knew you were from Whispering Slopes, but I thought you lived in Colorado."

Funny, that's what Meg had thought, too.

The woman scurried to Luke, practically tripping on her own feet. "I'm Tucker's teacher, Mrs. Cooper."

Luke smiled. "So, you're interested in bull riding?"

"Oh, yes. My husband and I love the rodeo. I always enjoy watching the mutton busting. The children are so cute with their big dreams of becoming a star like you."

Riding sheep. Meg shivered. That's how Luke and her father had gotten their start.

"Let's all have a seat over here at the table." Nick motioned to the round cherrywood furniture in the corner of the office. "Meg, just so you are aware, Tucker isn't being singled out today. The parents of the other student involved couldn't take off from work until tomorrow. I have their meeting scheduled." He glanced toward the boy. "Tucker, come and join us."

Meg's heart squeezed. All she wanted to do was take Tucker into her arms and tell him everything was going to be okay, but that would have to wait. She took a seat and patted her hand on the empty chair beside her. "Sit here, Tuck."

Nick swiped on his iPad and studied the screen before turning to the teacher. "Mrs. Cooper, can you share with us exactly what transpired today?"

The teacher cleared her throat. "Our class was outside with a few of the other classes for our morning break. It felt a little chilly to me, so I told one of the other teachers that I needed to step inside to grab my sweater. I heard yelling as I got closer to my classroom, which was odd since the children aren't permitted to go back inside unless accompanied by a teacher. Once in the room, I saw Tucker and Billy Johnson on the ground fighting." She paused and turned to Tucker, who still had his head down. "It appeared Tucker had Billy pinned underneath him."

"Is that true, Tucker?" The principal's brows drew together.

Seconds ticked past. Muffled giggles sounded outside in the hallway.

"Is that what happened?" Meg placed a comforting hand on Tucker's leg with hopes of getting him to open up and tell the truth.

He remained silent.

The adults all exchanged glances with each other before Principal Capello spoke. "Perhaps Mrs. Cooper can give us a little more insight?"

"From what I understand, the incident began earlier on the playground. Some of the other children heard Billy teasing Tucker before they saw him go inside the school. Apparently, Billy followed him a few moments later."

Meg's shoulders relaxed. At least some of the children came forward, otherwise it would have been Tucker's word against the other boy's. She looked down. "Is that the truth?"

Tucker's head gave a slight movement acknowledging the validity of his teacher's remarks.

That was all they were going to get out of him—at

least in front of an audience. Perhaps he'd open up to her later, at home. Meg took Tucker's hand and gave it a quick squeeze. She noted the dampness in his lashes.

The principal looked at Tucker. "I'm sorry you were teased, but you know fighting isn't the answer. You should have gone to Mrs. Cooper first and explained what happened, especially since it's against the rules to go back into the classroom without your teacher being present. As I mentioned, I plan to speak to Billy and his parents, too. I'll refrain from any disciplinary actions this time, but if you're caught fighting again, there will be consequences. I've already given you far too many warnings. Do you understand?"

"Yes, sir," Tucker whispered and bit his lower lip.

Meg appreciated Nick's decision. He was well aware Tucker struggled with his parents abandoning him and his sisters. But he'd given Tucker enough chances in the past. It was time her nephew learned how to walk away when he was teased instead of fighting.

"Thank you for your time, Mrs. Cooper. You and Tucker can return to the classroom. Please thank the aide for covering for you." Nick pushed away from the table and stood.

Tucker shot Meg a quick look. His expression was difficult to read. Was he upset with her? "I'll see you after school," she said as the child left the office with his teacher. Tucker lagged behind Mrs. Cooper, never looking back. Would she ever make progress with him? Somehow, she needed to find a way to reassure Tucker he was still loved despite the actions of his parents.

A piercing pain seared Luke's neck and moved down into his shoulder. The pills in his bathroom could be a fast and easy fix to dull the ache. A swift transformation to that feel-good state. He could begin preparing the walls with the primer he and Meg had picked up on their way home from the meeting with Tucker's principal. No. Pills would only temporarily mask the pain. They wouldn't get him back into competition. That was his goal—to continue to win before age forced him into retirement.

Then what?

He would once again be the unwanted son. And a grown man afraid to commit to a relationship with the only woman he'd ever loved. It was too late now. How could he expect unconditional love from Meg? Even his own father had told him he had nothing to offer her or anyone else.

He shook off the negative thoughts. His appointment had been rescheduled for tomorrow afternoon. The sooner he could address the injury, the faster he could return to the arena and keep winning—no matter how short-lived the euphoria, it gave Luke a sense of stability.

He scanned the walls in the largest room of Meg's B&B, the hawk's nest. Upon closer inspection of the damage from the storm, he concluded most of the drywall would need to be replaced before he could start painting.

Outside in the hallway, sounds of chatter moved closer. Tia and Tilly. Which one had the missing tooth? Tilly, wasn't it?

"I didn't know cowboys knew how to repair stuff." Tilly smiled and stepped into the room. Her eyes skimmed the ladder and painting materials.

No tooth. Definitely Tilly. "What? Do you think I only know how to ride horses?" Luke crossed his arms and smiled. With their curly hair pulled back into bouncy ponytails, both girls were adorable.

"Aunt Meg told us you hurt yourself and that's why you're here. We can help you fix the room. We might be little, but we're both pretty strong." Tilly moved closer.

"Til—Tuck said to stay away from him." Tia remained in the doorway with her hands behind her back.

So that explained the looks Tucker had thrown his way during the meeting at school. Tucker didn't trust him—or probably any adult. He couldn't blame the poor kid.

"That's nice of you to offer, Tilly, but your aunt Meg probably wouldn't want you in the middle of a construction job. It can be dangerous."

Tilly placed her hands on the back of her hips. "I'm not afraid of anything." Her brows knitted. "One day I'm going to be a rodeo star just like you. I want to be a barrel racer."

Luke struggled to keep a straight face. It was as though the proclamation had just popped into Tilly's head. But she appeared to be a tough little nugget. Who knew—one day she could become a barrel racer. Of course, Meg would never go for that. "So, you like to watch the rodeo?" He turned to Tia. "What about you? Do you like it, too?"

Tia shrugged her shoulders. "It's okay, I guess."

"Aunt Meg sure doesn't like it. She gets upset when I turn on the TV to watch." Tilly picked up a paintbrush and ran it along the palm of her hand.

"That's because of Grandpa, Til." Tia frowned.

Tilly looked up at Luke. "Yeah, our grandpa was famous like you." Her smile slipped away. "Some bad stuff happened and then he died."

Another reason to avoid the pills and seek the proper

treatment from Meg. Luke slipped his phone from his back pocket. The mood could use a lift. "Since you both like the rodeo, I'm sure you've heard of mutton busting." With a few taps of his phone, he pulled up a video.

"What's muffin busting?" Tilly crinkled her nose.

Luke laughed. "It's called mutton busting. Do you know what mutton is?"

The girls looked at each other and shrugged their shoulders simultaneously. "Nope." They responded in unison.

It was probably best to leave the meat out of his explanation. "I got my first taste of the rodeo when my uncle took me to watch mutton busting. Come take a look at this." He held out his phone and motioned for the children to come closer. "I was about your age." With one tap, the video started.

"They're sheep!" Tilly cried out, pointing to the device.

Tia giggled as the little boy hung on tight to the animal's underbelly.

"Oh, no, he's going to fall!" Tilly announced.

"Yeah, but he won't get hurt, Til. Sheep are short. It's not that far to the ground," Tia added.

Luke watched the girls. Their eyes were giant saucers as they looked at the screen in amazement. Exactly the reaction he'd had the first time he watched the sport live.

Tilly jumped up and down when the video ended. "Can we watch it again? Please!"

Tia clapped her hands. "Yes, please!"

Even Tia seemed to enjoy it. "I'll show you another one." He made a few taps, pulled up another film and pushed Play.

"That's a girl! I want to try it." Tilly pointed at the device.

"Try what, Til?" Everyone in the room turned and faced Tucker, who stood in the doorway. The joy that had filled the room faded.

Tucker's eyes burned in Luke's direction. He wasn't happy to see his sisters consorting with the enemy.

"Muffin busting! Come look, Tuck." Tia motioned her arm.

"It's mutton busting, Tia," Tilly corrected her sister.

The girls turned their attention away from Tucker and back to the video.

Tucker's feet remained firmly planted in place. He wasn't about to join his sisters.

Luke took notice of the familiar pain in Tucker's eyes. "Want to take a look, buddy?"

Tucker made a swift pivot on his heel and headed down the hallway.

Luke's focus remained on the empty doorway. *Lord, please show me a way to help Tucker.* Memories of his first trip to watch mutton busting with his uncle played in his mind. That day Luke had realized not all adults were like his parents. His uncle loved him for who he was, not for what he could do. Poor Tucker believed his parents had abandoned him because he wasn't good enough.

Luke turned to the girls, and an idea sparked. If they were reacting with this much enthusiasm, maybe it could be a way for him to connect with Tucker. Luke understood exactly how the boy felt. Even as an adult, Luke's pain still lingered.

Meg would have to agree to his plan, and she would be tough to convince. She despised anything rodeo. But he had to give it a try. The last thing Luke wanted was for Tucker to experience the same hurt he'd endured growing up. He wouldn't allow Tucker to believe he was unworthy of love.

Chapter Four

Early the following morning, parked in front of the B&B, Meg pressed her eyes closed and prayed for the engine to start. She turned the key in the ignition of her ten-year-old SUV for the fourth time. This was the last thing she needed this morning. *Come on. Start. Please.*

She didn't know much about cars, but she knew if the vehicle didn't start soon, she'd miss her first morning therapy appointment. With two sessions on her calendar before lunch, she didn't have time for this or the money it might cost her to get the problem repaired. Her fingers squeezed the steering wheel tighter.

Another expense. Unexpected expenses weren't a big deal when she'd lived alone. Now with three children dependent on her and a struggling second business— this was a very big deal. Leaning forward, she rested her head against the wheel and sent up a silent prayer.

"Not even a sputter. It looks like you might need a new battery."

Meg jumped at the deep voice coming through the half-opened passenger side window. She squinted into the morning sun. Luke's eyes were shielded by the dark brown cowboy hat that revealed just a glimpse of his dense eyelashes.

"Pop the hood for me." He moved from the window and patted his weathered, muscular hand on the front end of the car. A bull rider's hand. Just like her father's.

A glance at her watch told her she had under a half an hour to get to the office in time for the nine o'clock appointment. Meg pulled the lever, unlocking the hood. "Maybe you can give me a jump start? I've got an early session this morning."

Following a quick inspection, Luke slammed the hood closed and rounded the vehicle. His worn jeans swished as he moved in toward the driver's side window. "I think the battery is shot. It looks corroded. Any idea when it was last replaced?"

Long before her life had been turned upside down by her sister and brother-in-law deciding they could no longer take care of their children and business. "Honestly, I don't remember. Maybe five years ago."

"Come on." Luke opened the car door. "I'll drive you into town. I'm heading in to purchase some additional supplies to start work on the hawk's nest. I'll pick up a battery and install it myself."

The last thing Meg wanted was additional favors from Luke. She glanced toward the house. The children's toys riddled the front yard. Her shoulders dropped in defeat. "That would be a great help." Hiring an overpriced mechanic wasn't in her budget. But she couldn't allow Luke to do this for free. "I'll pay you for the battery and your time." She grabbed her bag off the passenger seat and stepped from the vehicle.

"Installing a battery is a cinch." Luke opened the passenger door of his oversize, bright red pickup truck. "Why don't I cover the cost of the materials I'm purchasing today, and we'll call it even?" A smile parted his lips.

Construction material was not cheap. "That doesn't sound fair to you," Meg said.

"If it makes you feel better, you can let me take you out to dinner sometime." He gave a quick wink and pushed the ignition button. The engine rumbled to life.

Wait. No way. Dinner out with Luke, the man who had broken her heart, was out of the question. She'd rather pay a high-priced mechanic—if only she had the money.

Ten minutes in, they rode in peaceful silence. Meg kept her eyes peeled on the road with her hands clasped together in her lap.

Luke eased his foot off the accelerator as the vehicle approached flashing red lights. The railroad crossing gate lowered, bringing the truck to a stop.

Meg turned her wrist to check the time and squirmed against the leather seat.

Luke turned to her. "Relax."

"I can't be late. I like to have plenty of time to review a new patient's file." She'd always been meticulous when it came to knowing every detail about her patients.

"You'll make it in plenty of time."

Boxcars passed in a blur. A lonesome whistle sounded, sending a shiver down Meg's spine.

"Still don't like that sound, do you?" Luke commented.

Meg shook her head. "It always reminded me of my father." Growing up, every night she would lie in her canopy bed and listen to the trains passing with hopes that one would bring her daddy home. "He was on tour so much. I don't think his family was a priority for him." Stability was something Meg had always craved. She wanted a normal family like her friends had. She would do everything in her power to provide the triplets with a stable home environment.

"That was his profession. It was how he provided for his family."

It was no surprise Luke would defend her father. Bull riders were a tight bunch. A fact Meg had learned early on. In a way, it was probably the only thing she'd ever liked about the profession.

Still, she couldn't recall a holiday where it was only her family celebrating together. Her father would always bring home a stray cowboy who didn't have a family of his own. One Thanksgiving, she'd hidden in her bedroom closet as her parents fought in the kitchen after her father surprised her mother with another mouth to feed. *Come on, Sue. He doesn't have anywhere else to go.* Meg always wondered if the nice man who'd ended up sharing their table had heard them arguing.

"I know he did his best. I just always wanted a traditional family. One that sat down to dinner each night and shared their day. Like yours."

The last few cars rumbled past, and the red light went dark. The gate opened with a jerky motion. "Things aren't always as they appear. You should know that from my letter." Luke turned his gaze back to the road.

Fifteen minutes later, Luke pulled up to the curb in front of Meg's office. "See, I got you here in plenty of time." He broke the silence that had filled the cab of the truck since they'd crossed the railroad track. She had no plans of discussing his letter today or any day.

"Thank you." Meg unfastened her seat belt and stepped from the vehicle.

"Anytime. If I'm your last appointment, we can ride home together."

Meg nodded. "You are." Since Meg's feet hit the floor this morning, she'd battled to keep thoughts of her therapy session with Luke today out of her mind. But that had proved to be as easy as starting a car with a dead battery.

"Do you feel comfortable with having your session at my office? I know you want to protect your privacy. If you'd rather do your physical therapy at the B&B, that would be fine by me." Whatever it took to treat Luke's injury. She wouldn't fail him like she had her father.

"I appreciate the offer, but I can park around back and hopefully slip inside unnoticed." Luke smiled.

Meg nodded. "Whatever you prefer."

"You won't be too hard on me, will you?" He flashed a smile through the open passenger door and unbuckled his seat belt.

Wait. Did he plan to come inside now? "No. I'll do an evaluation to determine the extent of your injury."

Luke jumped from the truck and rounded the vehicle. "Sounds like a plan. I'd love a cup of coffee—if you plan to make a pot. I didn't have a chance to get my caffeine fix this morning."

Meg looked up at Luke, who had more than twelve inches on her five-foot-three frame. When they were kids and everyone seemed to have a growth spurt except for her, Luke used to call her Shortstop. A soft breeze ignited a slight chill through her bones. Making coffee was the least she could do, but she'd have to keep the memories of their past at bay. "Sure, come on inside."

The office had plenty of daylight thanks to the floor-to-ceiling windows that covered one-half of the reception area. Meg was never one for fluorescent lighting. She moved toward the oak table positioned between two beige Queen Anne chairs and turned on the lamp. "I'll get the coffee brewing so you can go on with your day."

Meg headed toward the kitchenette. Luke trailed behind. "I'm not in a big hurry. The hardware store won't open for another half hour."

Meg busied her hands with the coffee pods, trying to ignore the familiar fresh, soapy scent wafting from Luke and straight in her direction. "You mentioned earlier that you planned to pick up drywall."

"Yeah, there's substantial water damage around the bedroom windows on the east side of the house. The wood needs to be replaced before I can start to paint."

Meg pressed the button on the coffee maker to brew the first cup. "I know I haven't evaluated the injury to your neck, but working with drywall doesn't sound like something you should be doing at this point…much less alone."

The machine hissed, and the aroma of coffee filled the small space. Meg opened the cabinet over the sink and removed a second cup. The appliance beeped, and she passed the full cup to Luke.

"Thank you." He took the beverage, and their fingers brushed. "I'm one step ahead of you on the project. I've reached out to an old rodeo buddy who lives outside town." Luke took a quick sip. "It tastes perfect. My friend Joe Carlson has offered to help. He plans to come by tomorrow morning."

One cowboy on the property was bad enough, but two? "I don't think that's a good idea." Meg removed the second brewed cup and turned off the machine. She stepped out into the reception area. Luke followed her lead.

"Joe is great with home repairs and remodeling."

Luke was prepared to argue his case. She wasn't in

the mood to discuss her financial situation with him for a second time, but he left her with no choice. "I can't have strangers working for free. And I don't have the money to pay your friend for his work."

"Don't worry about that. Joe owes me a few favors. Besides, he retired last year and he's driving his wife up the wall being under her feet around the house." Luke laughed. "You said it yourself, I shouldn't be working with the drywall by myself."

Meg moved toward the lateral file cabinet behind the front desk. She opened the drawer and removed the manila file with her first patient's documentation. She didn't have time to debate the issue. If Luke made his injury worse by helping her, she'd never forgive herself. Perhaps having Joe work with Luke would keep him safe and also get the repairs done sooner. After reviewing the B&B's books last night, she'd determined she needed to reopen at full capacity as soon as possible. "Okay, if Joe wants to help out, that's fine by me. But no more cowboys, okay?"

Luke chuckled. "You got it. Listen, I know you've got to prepare for your appointment, so I'll get out of your hair. But I did want to talk to you about taking the kids to a mutton busting competition that Joe mentioned. It's next weekend in Staunton. I thought we could make a day out of it."

Meg's shoulders stiffened, and the file she held dropped on top of the desk. "Absolutely not."

"But—"

"Luke. No. I don't want the children to have anything to do with that world—especially Tucker. Am I clear?"

Luke shoved his hands into the pockets of his jeans and nodded. "Understood. I'll see you later this afternoon for my appointment." He pivoted on his boot and exited the office.

Meg flopped into the leather desk chair and powered on the computer. Thoughts of her father swirled in her head. He'd shared stories of how his first experience watching mutton busting had planted the seed for him to become a rodeo star. And that was what he'd done. In the end, it destroyed her family and ultimately took her father's life way too soon. There was no way she would allow Luke to introduce the children to the rodeo circuit.

Before dawn on Thursday morning, Luke finished the last set of exercises Meg had shown him during their session yesterday afternoon. She'd printed off instructions that contained detailed diagrams of each of the movements that would help to speed the healing process.

Luke placed the sheet of paper on the dresser and ran his hand across the back of his neck. Meg had kept to the business at hand during his appointment, not allowing any personal discussions. He respected that. She was a professional. It was also obvious she didn't want any further mention of mutton busting. Although she had been adamant about her decision, he wasn't going to give up. Luke had a strong feeling it could be the answer to dealing with Tucker's abandonment issues.

Luke stepped out of his room. He had just enough time to grab a cup of coffee and head outside for a walk before Joe arrived to get started on the repairs.

"Mr. Beckett. Breakfast is being served in the dining room." Miss Mattie peered around the open door to the hallway linen closet.

Luke pulled his bedroom door closed. "Thank you, but I think I might just have coffee this morning."

Miss Mattie removed a stack of towels and pushed the door shut. "I don't mean to get into your business, but you need more than coffee, especially if you're going to start work on the rooms this morning. There's plenty of food for your friend, too." She smiled.

The aroma of crisp fried bacon drifted up the stairs from the kitchen. Luke's stomach rumbled in response. "That bacon does smell pretty good."

"Well, you better hurry along. It's Tilly and Tia's favorite. I'll be down in just a minute to serve you."

"Thanks for the heads-up, but don't rush on my account. I know my way around a kitchen pretty well." Suddenly ravenous, Luke scurried down the steps.

Soft giggles came from the kitchen. Luke took a quick peek around the corner. No sign of Meg. He debated whether it was appropriate to go inside. Despite his history with Meg, he was a guest, so he decided to make his way into the dining room and wait for Miss Mattie.

"Cowboy Luke!"

Before he had time to turn around, Tilly wrapped her arms around his leg. "We've been waiting for you to wake up. I thought cowboys got up extra early."

Tia kept her distance but smiled.

"Girls, let Mr. Luke have his breakfast in peace." Meg entered the room holding a coffeepot, her long hair swept up into a messy bun. Dressed in jeans and a pink T-shirt, she obviously wasn't headed to her office in town anytime soon.

"They're fine. I just hope they left me some of that delicious-smelling bacon."

Tilly giggled. "There's plenty. Tucker didn't eat any of his."

"You both need to go and brush your teeth. The school bus will be here in a few minutes." Meg crossed the room toward the table. "Have a seat, Luke. The coffee is fresh."

Luke pulled out the chair and sat down. Tilly ignored her aunt's instructions and jumped into the seat beside him. She placed her elbows on the table. "Can you show me and Tia some more of those funny videos?"

Tia shot across the room and took the empty seat on the other side of Luke.

Meg poured the coffee and set the pot on top of the place mat. She crossed her arms, and her brows drew together.

Busted. Yesterday when she'd nixed his idea of taking the kids to Staunton to watch some mutton busting, he'd never had an opportunity to mention he'd already given the children a little introduction to the competition.

"You can show Aunt Meg, too, Cowboy Luke." Tilly wiggled in her seat. "They are really funny."

Meg remained quiet.

Luke avoided eye contact with Meg. "I forgot to mention that I showed the kids some videos of mutton busting on my phone."

"Can we get some sheep, Aunt Meg? We've got two barns but no animals. What good are they empty? I want to try mutton busting. It looks like so much fun. And you don't have to worry about us getting hurt. The sheep are low to the ground." Tilly pleaded her case.

Luke looked up at Meg. "She has a good point." He grinned in an attempt to make light of the situation. He was aware of how Meg felt, and he respected that, but he didn't exactly agree with her.

"Will you at least watch the video?" Tilly gazed at her aunt while Tia remained quiet.

"I know all about mutton busting, so I don't need to watch any video. Now you girls go in the kitchen, get your brother and run upstairs and brush your teeth. I don't have time to drive you to school if you miss your bus."

"Tuck's not in the kitchen. He's still in bed for some reason." Tilly shrugged her shoulders and turned to Luke. "Maybe you can show us more videos later."

"Tilly—go," Meg commanded.

The children darted from the room.

"Is Tucker okay?"

Meg nodded. "I'm sure he's trying to get out of going to school again. He's been doing this more frequently."

"Do you think he's still being teased?"

"I wouldn't be surprised." Meg folded her arms across her chest. "I better go up and check on him. He can't miss any more school."

"Do you want me to go with you? I might be able to talk to him," Luke offered.

"I'm not trying to be rude, but I'd rather you didn't speak with Tucker. In fact, I'd rather you stay away from him as much as you can during your stay at the inn. I don't want him to get pulled into the world of cowboys or get too attached to you since you won't be staying permanently. I hope you understand. If you'll excuse me, I need to go talk to him and reassure him that he doesn't have to be afraid of the bullies at school."

Luke bit his tongue and nodded. This was the reason he believed strongly that introducing Tucker to mutton busting could help him gain confidence. Before his uncle took him to his first competition, Luke had been withdrawn from his family and friends. As much as he could understand the reasons behind Meg's reservations about Tucker getting involved in the rodeo world, he didn't agree with her. He'd have to figure out a way to change her mind.

Five minutes later, Luke had filled a travel mug with coffee, skipped the bacon and headed outside. Fresh air and a little distance between him and Meg was what he needed. She was just as stubborn as he remembered.

The warmth of the morning sunlight against his face cleared his jumbled mind. He followed the trail toward the largest barn, taking notice of the open field. It would be perfect for grazing. Tilly's words about having a barn with no animals came to mind. She was right. Given what the children had experienced after being abandoned by their parents, animals could help them get through the difficult situation of not feeling loved, just like Luke's horse and the other farm animals had helped him as a kid. Animals loved unconditionally— unlike his parents, who only paid attention to him when he brought home an award or medal.

As Luke continued down the path, a strange sound filled his ears. He came to an abrupt stop. A cloud of dirt kicked up behind his boots. He strained to listen. When the mockingbird on a nearby branch silenced, Luke heard the noise again. It was coming from the barn. Maybe some kind of animal? Curious, he stepped toward the structure to investigate. The last thing Meg needed was a family of skunks or opossums taking over the place.

The unusual noise grew louder when Luke reached the barn. The door squeaked as he carefully pushed it open. If it was a rabid fox or raccoon, he didn't want to scare it.

Across the floor, Luke spotted Tucker. He wasn't

upstairs in bed, after all. Luke remained quiet as he watched Tucker kick his foot against the door of one of the four empty stalls. He spoke to himself, but Luke wasn't able to make out what he was saying. Seconds later Tucker dropped to the ground and covered his eyes.

Luke stiffened. Had Tucker seen him? He never looked up, so maybe not. Meg had asked him to stay clear of Tucker, but the boy was obviously in distress. Luke didn't have the heart to just walk out and ignore what he'd witnessed.

"Tucker—can I come in?" Luke took one small step forward but stopped when the child looked up. There was minimal light inside the barn, but there was no mistaking the glistening tears that streamed down Tucker's flushed cheeks.

"Go away!" He shook his head.

Against his better judgment, Luke continued to move toward Tucker. Either he'd run away or refuse to talk, but Luke had to try. "You might feel better if you talk about what's bothering you."

Silence filled the space.

Luke sucked in a deep breath and advanced across the floor. "I know we don't really know each other yet, but I was hoping we could become friends."

Tucker wiped his eyes but didn't speak.

"I'm sure it's been hard for you being the only man around the house."

Tucker jerked his head upright. "I don't need your help! I can be the man of the house. It's what my daddy would want me to do."

Was this part of the problem? Tucker felt threatened by his presence. Maybe the boy believed Luke was trying to take his place as man of the house. "I'm sure you're doing a great job, but sometimes even the strongest man needs someone they can talk to."

Tears shimmered in Tucker's eyes. "Then how come my daddy didn't talk to me? Why would he just leave me?" he shouted. "He hasn't even called me. Do you think I did something to make him mad?"

Luke's parents had taken numerous business trips without so much as a goodbye. His uncle was left to make excuses, telling Luke it was last-minute or an urgent meeting. But at least they always returned. They might not have been there emotionally, but Luke didn't know the heartache of the physical void Tucker experienced. "Since I never knew your daddy, I can't really say. But I can promise you it wasn't because of anything you might have done."

Tucker rubbed his eyes. "He left the day before he'd promised to take me on a fishing trip. Just me and him. No girls. I had already packed my bag."

The situation was worse than he'd thought. Maybe Meg was right. He should have kept his distance. He had no experience with children, but he had decided to step inside the barn. There was no way he could leave Tucker, given his current state. "Do you mind if I sit?"

Tucker shrugged his shoulders.

Luke settled onto the wooden floor covered with a thin layer of hay. He picked up a piece of the straw and placed it between his lips. "Did you guys fish a lot together?"

Tucker's tears subsided for the first time. "Yeah, he said he always fished with his daddy, too."

"What did you like the best about it?" Luke hoped by prompting Tucker to talk about the good times he'd had with his father, it could ease some of his pain. At least for now.

"It was just us guys. No girls. He'd tell me stories about stuff he did when he was my age. And he always packed the best lunch." Tucker sighed. "I thought he liked to hang out with me."

Luke wished he could have two minutes with Tucker's father. What kind of man could do this? "I'm sure he loved to spend time with you. Do you know what I think?"

Tucker shrugged his shoulders.

"Maybe your father had some problems he didn't want to trouble you with."

Tucker's brow crinkled. "Maybe—but now I don't have anyone to talk to."

"You have your aunt Meg and your sisters. They're your family. They're not going anywhere."

Tucker shook his head. "It's not the same. I can't talk to them about guy stuff. They wouldn't understand."

Luke knew he was going against Meg's wishes, but his heart was heavy for Tucker. "You can talk to me. I can be a pretty good listener."

"But you're only here for a visit. You'll be leaving, just like my daddy."

Luke considered Tucker's comment. The child wanted stability. It was exactly what he had craved as a young boy. What he still craved. Rodeo life was exciting and the adrenaline rush was hard to match, but there was no room for permanency. No room for a family. Or a home. "But once I'm gone, we can always talk on the phone. Maybe we could even do a video chat. Let's not think about me leaving. I'll be around for at least the next six weeks. We could do a lot of cool stuff together during that time."

Tucker palmed his face. No more tears. This was good. Luke placed his hand on the boy's shoulder.

"What do you say? I could use a little guy time, too. There's a lot of girls in that B&B, huh?" He winked, and for a moment, Luke saw the child's face brighten, but only for a second.

"Okay. But just me and you. No girls, right?"

Luke laughed. "Absolutely." Outside the barn the rumbles of an engine sounded. Luke glanced at his watch. As usual, Joe was right on time to start work on the hawk's nest. "Now, come on. Let's head back to the house. Your aunt Meg will have my hide if you miss the bus." Luke stood and reached out his hand to help Tucker off the ground.

Tucker remained silent when he looked up at Luke, as though he was questioning whether or not to put his trust into another adult. His thick, lashes fluttered. "Thanks for making me feel better."

A warmth filled Luke's heart. "I'm here whenever you need to talk. Okay?"

Tucker nodded, pulled his hand free, and strolled through the open barn door. Luke raked his hand across the top of his head. The desire to help Tucker cope with the loss of his parents had caught him off guard. Going against Meg's wishes was wrong, but the moment he'd felt Tucker's tiny hand in his own and captured a hint of his smile, Luke knew he was doing the right thing.

Chapter Five

Meg's shoulders relaxed when she stepped out onto the front porch and spotted Tucker coming out of the barn as a pickup truck traveled down the gravel driveway. She'd spent the last fifteen minutes scouring the B&B, looking in all Tucker's favorite hiding places. The barn. She should have known to check there first. Poor Tucker. Despite all her prayers, Meg had been unable to have a breakthrough with her nephew. He carried around so much anger, but Meg knew deep down the child's heart had been broken into tiny pieces after being abandoned by both parents.

Tucker looked up, and his eyes glinted. He took off running and reached the porch steps, taking them two at a time. "Sorry, Aunt Meg. I'll get my backpack."

Meg crossed her arms and watched Tucker head into the house. She quickly turned at the sound of the truck's door slamming and then voices. The relaxed feeling she'd had after seeing Tucker was safe vanished when she spotted Luke coming out of the barn. He'd found her nephew.

Luke spoke to the slightly gray-haired man with a tall yet slim build. He patted him on the shoulder and turned toward the house. Meg's shoulders straightened as Luke approached the porch steps.

Luke rested his hand on the railing. "That's my friend Joe. I'll introduce you after he unloads some of his tools."

Meg nodded. She forced herself to let go of the tension building. Tucker was safe, and that was most important. Now wasn't the time to get into a discussion about boundaries for Luke and the children, yet she was curious about what had transpired in the barn. "Thanks for finding Tucker. I should have known to check the barn."

"No problem. When I heard some noises coming from inside, I went to investigate." He tapped the tip of his boot into the side of the porch. "I know you asked me to try and keep some distance from the children, but once I heard him crying, I couldn't leave him alone."

Meg's heart sank. For over a year, she'd tried to do the right thing for the kids. Tia and Tilly seemed to have adjusted to the void of having been left behind by their parents, but that wasn't the case for Tucker. No matter how hard she tried, Meg had been unable to get him to open up to her. She'd even considered getting a professional involved. "Did he tell you why he was upset? I can't get him to talk to me about his feelings."

Luke sank his hands into the front pockets of his jeans. "He's really struggling."

The children would be coming outside to catch the bus, and she didn't want them to overhear the conversation. She moved closer to the top of the steps. "What did he say?"

"He seems to think he did something that caused his parents to leave."

Meg wrapped her arms tight around her stomach.

She was afraid of this. In hindsight, it was exactly how she had felt when she was young and her father would leave to go on tour. She'd often questioned whether or not her father would have stayed around more if she did better in school or kept her room cleaner. As an adult, she was able to accept or at least understand why her father had left the family, but a young mind could dream up all kinds of reasons. Most of which mistakenly blamed the child. "Poor Tucker. I knew he missed his parents, but I didn't know he carried around this guilt."

"I think it's harder for him than it is for the girls because he always thought he and his father were a team." Luke squinted into the morning sun.

"Boys against girls?"

He nodded. "Something like that. He's hurt because his father didn't come and talk to him. But worst of all, his father left the night before he had promised to take Tucker on a fishing trip. Just the guys."

The coffee Meg had drunk earlier soured in her stomach. "I had no idea." And here she'd thought she'd done a halfway decent job stepping into the role of mother to the triplets. Had she made the situation worse by not insisting her sister continue to seek professional help?

"I know what you're thinking—but don't. You're doing a great job with the children. Tucker's situation is different from the girls'." Luke turned toward Joe's truck. "I'd like to talk some more about this, but I need to help Joe unload his equipment so we can get to work upstairs."

Meg raked her hand through the back of her hair. "You're right. The kids' bus will be here soon. I'd like to talk some more about Tucker, too. I need to figure out a way to help him. I'd rather have the discussion when the children aren't around."

Joe approached the porch carrying an oversize toolbox. He placed it on the ground.

"Meg, this is an old friend of mine, Joe Carlson." Luke made the introduction.

"It's nice to meet you, Joe. I appreciate you helping Luke with the repairs. Can I get you some coffee or anything to drink?" Meg offered.

"That's nice of you, but I'm fine. It's a pleasure to meet you, ma'am." Joe tipped his cowboy hat and turned to Luke. "I'm going to run back to the truck and wait for you so we can get the table saw unloaded. Do you want to cut the drywall out on the driveway?"

Luke nodded. "That would probably be the best place since it will be messy with the dust. I'll be there in a minute."

Joe headed back to the vehicle.

"About that talk—do you want to grab a late lunch this afternoon after my therapy session?" Luke suggested.

"That'll work. You're my last appointment for the day. Miss Mattie will be here to meet the children when they get off the bus."

"Do you mind if we go someplace outside town? You know how the rumor mill is. All it will take is for one person to see us dining together and the entire town will be planning our wedding." Luke laughed. "It feels like we're doing something illegal."

Meg laughed. "It does."

"It all seems kind of silly, doesn't it? It's not like I'm a famous movie star."

"Maybe not, but you are the top bull rider in the country. And the fact that you're from Whispering

Slopes makes you famous around here." Meg considered Luke and his life. She couldn't help but wonder where the two of them would be today if he hadn't left town. If he had chosen a life with her over a career in the spotlight. She shook off the thought. No sense dwelling on the past. *What's done is done.* "I better check on the kids. Please don't overdo it with the drywall project today."

Luke gave a salute. "Yes, ma'am. I'll be careful. Actually, my neck is feeling pretty good. I think the exercises you gave me are working." Luke smiled and rubbed his hand along the back of his neck.

"I'm glad to hear that, but it's going to take more than a day or two of doing the exercises to heal your injury. It's not something you should take lightly."

"I get the message. I better go help Joe. So, I'll see you at one o'clock for my session."

"Sounds good."

"That will give me a good four hours to work on the room. Are you okay with Joe working alone after I leave? Trust me, he's as honest as they come." Luke smiled again.

"Sure, that's not a problem." Meg watched as Luke headed toward the truck. She was happy he had some help, but she still wasn't comfortable with him doing strenuous activities this early in his recovery. But being the typical strong-willed bull rider, he'd insisted everything would be fine.

Perhaps it was for the best. The faster Luke could get her rooms repaired and recover from his injury, the sooner he'd head back to Colorado. But she refused to allow him to go back on the circuit without doing her part to help the healing process. She'd let it happen with her father. She wouldn't repeat the same mistake.

* * *

Luke settled into a booth toward the back of Ma-maw's Country Kitchen, a roadside diner fifteen miles outside the Whispering Slopes town limits. The place had been around as long as he could remember. The food had always been great. He'd read some good reviews of the place online, so he'd suggested they meet there since Meg had a quick errand to run after his session. Would she remember it had been the spot of their first date back in junior high school? Or had she permanently erased their time together? Her dismissing any discussion of the letter suggested the latter.

With the lunch hour coming to a close, and only a few customers scattered around the restaurant, Luke hoped there would be fewer rodeo fans. A strong aroma of grilled onions filled the air—a reminder that he'd passed on breakfast and was now ravenous. A steak-and-cheese sub sandwich would hit the spot.

Luke gazed out the smudged window, admiring the emerging wildflowers coming to life and reaching for the sun along the mountainside. Growing up, he'd always looked forward to spring. Not only because the warmer weather allowed him more time outside, but because it was the time of year when he was always most hopeful for change. Always thinking this could be the year that his parents would love him as much as his older brothers.

Moments later, gravel crunched in the parking lot. Meg's white SUV glided into an empty spot next to his truck. Luke watched as Meg exited her vehicle. The ponytail she'd worn during his therapy session was gone and replaced with wavy blond strands flowing beyond her shoulders. She reached for her purse, closed the door and hurried toward the restaurant.

"Sorry, I got caught at the railroad crossing." Meg slid into the booth, leaned back and looked around. "I haven't been here in ages."

Luke scanned the room and placed his arms on the table. "Do you think Mamaw still runs the place?"

"No. She passed away about five years ago. Her granddaughter took over. I'm glad they've kept it in the family, though." Meg paused, and their eyes connected. "I'm curious—what made you pick this place?"

She remembered. Was that a good thing or bad? As a nervous teenager, he recalled fumbling on his words and knocking over her soda ten minutes into the date. Thankfully she had fast reflexes and jumped up before the brown liquid had covered her white jeans.

"I don't know. Maybe I was feeling a bit nostalgic for the old days." Luke fingered the red plastic menu in front of him.

Meg's brow furrowed. "I thought you wanted to leave that time in the past."

"What makes you say that?"

She straightened her shoulders. "The way you bolted out of town. I thought you'd never want to step foot across the state line again."

Meg's words ushered in a rush of emotions. That summed up his actions perfectly. He had bolted. Following an argument where his father denied ever treating Luke differently than his brothers and said he'd never be a good provider for Meg. His father's words had stung. *You're just a rodeo star wannabe with a few trophies.* Luke had packed his bag and decided that night to carry out his plan to leave town. The one glitch in the plot had been not sitting down to explain the reason for his departure to Meg. How could he when she was part of the reason he chose to leave? That's when he decided to try and explain it on paper. "I told you everything in the letter."

"Right—the letter." She picked up her menu. "We better get our order in so we can discuss what we came here to talk about."

The cold stare Meg shot his way made it obvious she hadn't forgiven him. Had his words in the letter meant nothing to her? Had she ever really cared about him? Sure, he'd only been a teenager, but he'd poured his heart out on those pages. He'd revealed feelings he'd never shared with anyone. Those painful words spoken to him by his father and still fresh today had confirmed everything he'd ever believed about his parents—he'd been a surprise pregnancy to them and one they never wanted.

"You're right. We're here to talk about the kids."

The young waitress approached their table and froze. "I can't believe it," she squealed. "You're Luke Beckett." Her hand shook as she placed two glasses on the table and filled each with water. "I'm a huge fan." The woman's cheeks flushed. "I know this sounds silly, but could I have your autograph? My boyfriend is a big fan of yours, too, and he'll never believe me when I tell him that I waited on you." She set the pitcher back on her tray and pulled a pencil from behind her ear.

Luke had never turned down a request for an autograph. "Sure." He plucked a napkin from the holder.

"My name is Jenny," she giggled.

Luke jotted his usual message and handed her the paper.

Jenny read the autograph and smiled. "Thank you so much." She folded the napkin in half and slid it into the pocket of her yellow apron. "Do you need a few more minutes or are you ready to order?"

"Do you know what you'd like?" Luke directed his question to Meg.

"I'll have a grilled cheese sandwich and a cup of chicken noodle soup." Meg closed the menu and placed it on the table.

"And for you?" the waitress asked as she scribbled Meg's order on her pad.

"My mouth has been watering for a steak-and-cheese sub ever since I stepped through the door and smelled those sweet onions." Luke picked up Meg's menu and passed them along. "And a side of onion rings, too."

"You got it. Anything to drink?" The woman slipped the order pad into the other pocket of her apron.

"Water's fine for me," Meg answered.

Luke nodded. "Same here."

"I'll get your order in right away." She scurried off toward the kitchen.

Luke smiled. "I see you still love grilled cheese."

Meg's posture appeared to relax for the first time since she'd entered the restaurant. "I guess it's my turn to be nostalgic."

"You would have eaten those sandwiches every day if your mother would have allowed it."

"That's one of the bonuses of being an adult—you get to decide the menu each night." She smiled. "Before I came back to Whispering Slopes, I used to eat grilled cheese and soup practically every night."

Luke leaned in. "And now?"

"Every Friday night. Thankfully, the kids love it, too. Of course, I have to be a grown-up and feed them a well-balanced diet." Meg ran her finger down the condensation on the side of her water glass. "When I was young, I always thought how great it would be to be an adult and make all the rules."

Luke couldn't imagine how much Meg's life had changed. First her brother-in-law left and then her sister followed his lead and abandoned their children. Meg had inherited the B&B and a lot of financial responsibilities. In an instant, her world had been turned upside down. "You should be proud of what you've done. Stepping in and giving up your practice in Richmond to give the children some stability is admirable."

"Don't make me out to be a hero."

"Overnight, you became a mother and a business owner. That's a lot. I'm not so sure I would have been able to do what you've done." Luke's hand moved across the table but then retreated.

Sunlight streamed through the window, putting a spotlight on the tears brimming in Meg's eyes. "After my father died, Gina was all the family I had left. I knew what it felt like to grow up in an unstable environment. I couldn't allow the triplets to feel the same. Besides, I made a promise to Gina to keep the B&B open for the sake of the children." She wiped her eyes. "But it looks like history is repeating itself. My life is anything but stable."

"You're just dealing with some unexpected circumstances right now. Once the repairs are completed at Trout Run, your business will be booming. I promise."

"First I have to get out from under the enormous amount of debt Gina and Greg left behind, but I need to be realistic. Having a successful business isn't going to be the balm for Tucker's broken heart. He's hurting, and I'm at my wit's end as to how I can help him."

If Luke didn't address the topic now, there would probably not be another opportunity. "Tucker is hurting pretty bad right now."

Meg squirmed in the booth. "Can you tell me more about what you two spoke about in the barn?"

Luke watched as their waitress ferried their food across the floor of the restaurant and motioned his head in her direction. "Sure, but after we eat."

The waitress placed the order on the table. "Is there anything else you need?"

Meg shook her head.

"I think we're good. Thank you." Luke unwrapped his silverware and placed the napkin on his lap as the waitress headed to a neighboring table. "Let's eat. I'm starving."

Twenty minutes later the plates had been cleared and the small talk had come to a close. Luke patted his stomach. "I don't think I'll need to eat until breakfast tomorrow. That was delicious."

"Mamaw's always had the best grilled cheese." Meg blotted her lips with the napkin. "Can we talk about Tucker?"

"Yes, but I'd rather keep this conversation between the two of us. I might have earned a little of Tucker's trust this morning, or at least I hope that I did. I wouldn't want to lose it by having you question him about anything I tell you. At least for now," Luke requested.

"If you think it will help him."

Luke nodded. "Of course, if he ever mentions anything to me that could cause him harm in any way, you'll be the first to know. I've asked him if he wants to hang out with me—just the guys."

"I'm not so sure that's a good idea since you'll be leaving."

"Funny, that's the same thing Tucker mentioned."

Meg folded her arms and pressed her back firmly against the booth. "If he gets attached and then you leave, how will that help with his feelings of being abandoned? I don't want to cause him any additional heartache."

"Believe me, I understand where you're coming from. But I think I can help him work through some of his pain."

Meg's brow crinkled. "But you hardly know Tucker. I've been trying to get him to talk to me for the past year, and I've gotten nowhere."

"That's exactly my point. Maybe it's time to try a different strategy." Luke inhaled a deep breath and slowly released it. "I'd like your permission to spend some time with him. Just me and Tucker. Would you be all right with that?"

A group of elderly women entered the restaurant. Laughter filled the air as they settled into a nearby table.

Meg waved to the group and turned her attention back to the discussion. "I guess that all depends on what you plan to do."

Anything but something rodeo related. That's what Meg was thinking, but he believed it would help Tucker. "I'd like to take him to the mutton busting competition. The one in Staunton next weekend. I know I mentioned you and I taking the triplets, but I think it might be a good idea for Tucker and me to go alone." Luke sucked in a breath and prepared for the worst.

Her lips pursed. "I thought I'd made myself clear. I don't want any of the children to have anything to do with the rodeo. It's hard enough for me to keep them from watching it on television when a guest turns it on in the gathering room."

"I know that's what you said, and I understand. But please, let me take Tucker just this one time. I honestly believe it will be good for him."

"Why can't you just take him fishing or something?

Why does it have to be rodeo related?" Meg fingered the gold chain around her neck.

"If you could have seen the girls when I showed them the video of the mutton busting competition, you might feel differently. Maybe it was wrong of me to do that without your permission, but at the time I guess I wasn't thinking."

"What if Tucker loves it?"

"Would that be such a bad thing?"

"It would be if it drives him to want to become a professional bull rider like you."

Ouch. Meg definitely had no love for his profession. Of course, he understood her reasons. "I don't think attending one event would convince Tucker to make that his career goal. He's only six years old." Luke laughed in an attempt to lighten the mood.

Meg leaned back and crossed her arms. "I can't believe you're saying that. You told me years ago about your first childhood rodeo experience with your uncle and the impact it had on you. The impact I'm sure it still has on you."

He couldn't argue with her there. It was true. But he had to at least try and have a breakthrough with Tucker. He couldn't allow the boy to continue to believe he was the reason his parents left.

"Let me take him just this once. I promise I won't ask you again."

"You know I've seen firsthand the lure rodeos can have on people, particularly little boys. My father's profession destroyed my family. I don't want Tucker to go down that same path."

Luke needed to think fast or Meg was going to completely shut the door. "How about a compromise? We go with my original plan. You, me and the kids all go together as a family. You'll be there to keep an eye on Tucker, so he doesn't run off and join the tour."

Meg considered the offer, and her shoulders slumped. "Okay, but only this one time." She looked at her watch. "I better get home."

A few minutes later, behind the wheel of his truck, Luke replayed the conversation. In his heart he knew Meg had every reason to not want Tucker to attend the competition. But he wasn't worried that the boy would want to join the rodeo circuit after one mutton busting competition. His bigger concern was the offer he'd made to Meg back at the diner. Going to the event as a family. Was that what he wanted? A family of his own?

Luke brushed off the thought. He was in Whispering Slopes to recover, and then he'd head back to Colorado and keep doing what he knew best—winning. Rodeo life supplied him with the income to have the stability he had always wanted, not family life. No. He needed to stick to the plan.

Chapter Six

Meg reduced the flame underneath the skillet. Since Miss Mattie had the day off on Saturday, Meg had planned a big breakfast before they headed out to Staunton. Her stomach squeezed. Why had she allowed Luke to talk her into taking the children to the mutton busting competition? She had regretted her decision the moment she'd agreed. But it was too late now. The children knew they were going someplace special, but Luke had asked that they keep exactly where a secret.

"That bacon sure smells delicious." Luke peeked his head into the kitchen. "Do you need some help?"

"I think I have everything under control, but if you want to set the table, that would be nice." She pointed to the cabinets next to the kitchen sink. "The plates are in there and the silverware is in the drawer below."

"You got it."

Meg watched Luke move across the kitchen and open the cabinet. He removed five plates and carried them to the table.

"I guess we'll just eat in here," he suggested.

Uncertainty bubbled. Luke was a guest, and guests always ate in the dining room. But he had a point. Since it was just him and the kids it didn't make much sense. The children were used to eating in the kitchen. "Sure."

"So, the kids still don't know where we're going today, right?"

"No, they don't, but it sure hasn't been from a lack of trying. Since I mentioned we were going somewhere, the girls have been hounding me to find out where we are taking them. You'd think it was Christmas morning."

Luke laughed. "And Tucker?"

Meg shrugged. "Not a peep. He hasn't shown any interest in wanting to go." Meg couldn't help but wonder if perhaps Luke's idea was a good one after all. Nothing else she had tried seemed to be working.

"Hang on, he'll come around." Luke rested his hand on her shoulder as she stood at the stove.

Caught off guard by his touch, she jumped.

"I'm sorry." He stepped back and moved toward the silverware drawer.

"I hope you're right. If something doesn't change soon, I'm going to have to make an appointment for us to go and talk to someone. I know Tucker won't like that. He'll hardly talk in front of his principal, so I can't imagine what he'd be like being questioned by a stranger."

Luke folded five napkins and placed them along with the silverware on the table. "I don't think it'll come to that. I have a good feeling about our outing today. I guarantee you're going to see a big change in Tucker by the end of the day."

Excited chatter filled the air as Tilly and Tia galloped into the kitchen.

"Cowboy Luke! Are you going to eat with us, too?" Tilly grinned.

"As a matter of fact, I am. Your aunt was kind enough

to invite me to join you guys so I don't have to eat alone in the dining room." Luke glanced in Meg's direction.

Tilly jumped up and down. "This is going to be the best day ever!"

Tia shot her sister a questioning look. "But you don't even know where we're going, Til."

"I know, but if Cowboy Luke is taking us, I know it'll be fun." She twirled on her heels.

Luke gazed at Meg and winked. A spark of nostalgia ignited as she recalled him doing the same gesture when he'd drop her off after driving her home from school. Meg relaxed when she spied Tucker entering the kitchen. She struggled to pull her stare off the handsome cowboy.

Tilly ran toward her brother. "Tuck, Aunt Meg is making your favorite—bacon. She's even cooking blueberry pancakes."

Tucker kept his eyes down to avoid contact with everyone in the room, his face void of expression.

Meg's heart broke for her nephew. He'd been happy after he and Luke had spoken in the barn, but maybe he'd realized the reality of the situation. Luke's stay wasn't permanent. She longed for the excited child she remembered during past holiday visits before his parents abandoned their children. She reduced the flame underneath the skillet and approached him. "Are you excited for our surprise outing today?"

"I am!" Tilly took it upon herself to answer. "I couldn't sleep a wink."

Tucker remained silent as everyone watched him. His head slowly lifted toward Meg. "Can I stay here with Miss Mattie today?"

"You know she doesn't work on Saturday, Tuck."

Tilly frowned and placed her hands on her hips. "Come on. We're going to have so much fun today."

Tucker moved closer to Meg. "But my tummy doesn't feel good."

Meg didn't want to be cruel, but she had to trust Luke and his idea to bring a little joy into Tucker's life. "I'm sure you'll feel better after you have a little breakfast. I promise you'll have a good time today."

Tucker spun on his heel, headed to the table and flopped into the chair. He kept his head down for the entire meal, hardly eating a bite and never speaking a word.

Watching the boy suffer was more than she could bear. Now it was her stomach that wasn't feeling so good.

Later that morning, Meg's heartbeat accelerated as Luke navigated his truck into the crowded parking lot of the Staunton arena.

"Are we going to the circus?" Tilly called out from the back seat of the extended cab.

"It's a surprise, remember? You'll have to wait and see," Luke answered as he pulled into a space and placed the vehicle in Park.

Meg stepped out of the truck and opened the back door. Luke followed her lead. The girls unfastened their seat belts and bounded from the vehicle, but Tucker stayed inside. She'd been afraid this would happen. He'd done this a few times after he missed the bus and she'd driven him to school. He'd sit quietly inside the car and refuse to move. Meg leaned in. "Come on Tuck, we're here. Let's go have some fun."

A few seconds passed before the boy reluctantly complied.

They walked at a brisk pace with Luke leading the way into the arena. Meg and the children followed.

Tilly pulled her hand away from Meg and skipped forward. She reached for Luke's hand, looked up at Luke and smiled. Something told Meg she should have never agreed to this outing.

Country music blasted from the speakers overhead as they entered the arena. The expansive space had been divided into multiple seating areas, each equipped with bleachers and metal fencing surrounding dirt-covered floors. Although indoors, it felt as though you were outside. As Meg continued to take in her surroundings, she realized this wasn't only a mutton busting competition.

Tilly grabbed her sister's arm and jumped up and down. "It's the rodeo, Tia! Just like we watch on television. This is going to be so awesome!"

Meg shot a look at Tilly. Those were Meg's exact thoughts. Not the awesome part, but if she had known this was where Luke planned to bring them, she never would have agreed. Meg reached for Luke's arm and pulled him aside. "You failed to mention the surprise was a rodeo. I thought it was simply a mutton busting competition." How could he do this to her? He'd completely gone against her wishes.

"I'm sorry. I didn't know. Joe never mentioned anything other than the competition. He knew how much I enjoyed it as a child." Luke ran his hand across his face. "Since we're already here and the kids are so excited, let's try to have a good time."

Meg stood frozen. She didn't have a good feeling about this at all.

"Come on, Aunt Meg. There's so much to see—we can't waste time standing around here." Tilly yanked on her arm, while Tucker displayed no sign of interest. This wasn't the outcome she'd prayed for.

The girls were excited, she got that. The last thing she wanted to do was to disappoint them. After Luke had convinced her to bring the children today, she'd had hopes it would bring Tucker a little joy in his life. Maybe attending the event wouldn't make him want to join the rodeo. At least she prayed that would be the case. Still, being here was stirring up old memories of her father. Ones she'd rather forget.

After Meg had given the okay to go ahead and check out some of the events, Luke breathed a sigh of relief. He'd gotten over that hurdle. Yet the biggest challenge was to get Tucker interested. He hadn't taken his eyes off the ground since they'd stepped inside the arena. Of course, Tilly and Tia were making up for his lack of enthusiasm.

"Can we go to the petting zoo, Cowboy Luke?" Tilly looked up, her cheeks rosy with excitement.

Luke's heart melted. He loved seeing her so happy, but he longed for Tucker to feel the same way.

"I want to see the baby goats." Tilly looked at her sister, who smiled. "Tia wants to go, too. It doesn't matter about Tucker. He'll go wherever we want to go. He doesn't care."

Tilly's words stung. Luke was more determined than ever to have his breakthrough with Tucker today. He turned to Meg. "How does that sound? Is the petting zoo okay with you?" It was probably the most non-rodeo-related event at the show.

Meg nodded. "Sure, that might be educational for the children."

Luke raised his right brow. "What about the kids

having a little plain old fun? Everything in life doesn't have to be like school." He stepped closer and nudged his shoulder against hers. "Come on. Let's go and have some fun."

They moved through the crowded venue. An aroma of manure and hay filled the air.

"Look!" Tilly pointed across the way. "There's cows over there. We have two barns and tons of land, can we get some cows, Aunt Meg?"

Luke tried to bypass the look Meg shot his way. "Let's just enjoy the animals here today. Owning cows, horses and goats is a big responsibility."

They reached the metal fencing that surrounded the petting area. Luke approached an elderly man wearing a name tag. He stood next to a table filled with ice cream cones. "Can the adults go in, too, or is this just for children?"

"Oh, no, everyone is welcome inside. This area only houses the smaller animals."

Never fearing a stranger, Tilly marched up to the older gentleman. "We want to see the baby goats," she proclaimed.

The man laughed. "Well, you've come to the right place. We also have llamas, alpacas and some piglets."

Tilly's eyes zeroed in on the table filled with her favorite dessert. "Are the ice cream cones for us?"

"They're actually for the animals." He picked up a cone and showed her the contents. "Each cone has sunflower seeds, raisins and pellets. This is all safe food for you to feed the animals."

"Wow! I thought we could only pet them. We can feed them, too?" Tilly jumped up and down. "Did you hear that, Tia?"

The older man laughed. "Sure, they love to be hand-fed. Just don't feed the pigs, since they have teeth like humans. You can still pet them, though."

"It sounds like you have a little bit of everything." Luke scanned the fenced area.

"We do. We like to give the children a firsthand experience of what it's like to live on a farm. None of the animals are in cages of their own. They are all free to walk around with each other."

Luke looked over at Tucker. There was still no sign of interest from the boy. Luke reached for a cone from the table and stepped toward Tucker, who stood with his back turned against the animals. "Hey, buddy. Do you want to come in with me and feed the llamas? Even though they're related to the camel, they probably won't spit on you." Luke laughed in an attempt to get Tucker to smile, or at least show a little interest in the animals.

Tucker slowly turned around. "I thought we were going to do something alone. Just the guys."

So that's why he'd been so quiet at breakfast. Guilt consumed Luke. He had told Tucker they could hang out together without the girls around. That's what Tucker had enjoyed doing with his father. "You're right. Let me talk to your aunt Meg."

When Luke approached, Meg was busy gathering cones for the girls, who were preoccupied petting a goat through the fencing. "Can I talk to you for a second?"

"Sure, what's up?"

He inhaled a breath. *The worst she can say is no.* "Would it be okay with you if I show Tucker around?" Luke noticed Meg's back straighten.

"I'm not sure if that's a good idea."

Luke rested his hand on Meg's arm. "Don't worry, we're only going to do a little exploring."

"Just the guys?" Meg gave an understanding nod and

smiled. "Well, I think that will be okay. I can take the girls inside to pet some of the animals." Meg scanned her surroundings and looked at her watch. "Why don't we meet at the food court in an hour or so? Is that okay with you?"

"Great. Thank you so much. You won't be sorry."

Meg moved toward Tucker and placed her hand under his chin. "Do you want to go with Mr. Luke while I take your sisters into the petting zoo area?"

Tucker nodded several times.

This was a good start. "Are you ready to go have some fun?" Luke reached his hand out to the boy.

Tucker kept both arms glued to his side as he looked up. Slowly he extended his hand and placed it in Luke's grip. Yes, this was progress.

A short walk later, Luke and Tucker settled into the metal bleachers that surrounded a dirt-covered circular arena. "You're going to love this." Luke smiled at Tucker, who sat stiff and stared ahead.

"Remember the other day when I was showing the girls a video on my phone?"

Tucker nodded.

"Well, you're about to see the real thing live right down there." Luke tilted his head toward the ring. "When I was your age, my uncle brought me to an event like this. It's called mutton busting."

"What are those sheep doing over there?" Tucker directed his finger toward a gathering of four sheep.

"They're waiting their turn to go into the chute. See that man over there? He's called a handler. In a few minutes, he's going to help a boy or a girl about your age onto a sheep that is brought into that chute."

"What for?"

Asking questions was a good sign. "So they can ride

the animal and see how long they can stay on. Most kids fall off in the first few seconds."

Tucker shrugged his shoulders and crinkled his brow. "I could probably go longer than that."

Luke laughed. That's exactly what he'd thought, but he found out early, it wasn't as easy as it looked.

A young boy walked across the arena, and the crowd cheered.

"Why is he wearing a helmet?" Tucker questioned.

"It's to protect his head when he falls off. They don't want anyone to get injured. Even though it's not a far drop, they don't want to take a risk."

"I don't think I would need one since I wouldn't fall."

Luke stifled a laugh. He'd been just as confident his first time on the back of a sheep. With each tumble, he was more determined the next time. He could only hope Meg would come around and allow Tucker to give it a try. He'd find out just like Luke had that mutton busting was harder than it looked. "Helmets are mandatory, buddy."

The handler placed the boy on the sheep's back.

"Keep an eye on the door to the chute. Once that opens, the action starts." Luke watched Tucker as he inched toward the edge of his seat.

The gate swung open, and the sheep rocketed out of the chute with the boy hugging its underbelly, trying to hang on. In under three seconds, the sheep won. The child tumbled to the ground but jumped up, flashed a big smile and waved as the crowd cheered him on.

Luke's heart soared at the sound of Tucker's laughter—something he hadn't heard before. Tucker looked up to Luke, a smile stretched from ear to ear. Yes. This was exactly the reaction he'd been praying for.

"That was the coolest thing ever! I want to see it again." Tucker sprang to his feet and craned his neck.

Luke could barely contain his joy. "Hang on, buddy, there'll be another one coming out in just a minute."

Tucker kept his eyes peeled on the first contestant as he circled the arena smiling and waving to the crowd.

Luke recalled the feeling even though it was so many years ago. Just hanging on for a couple of seconds felt like such an accomplishment. It was a dream come true.

Once the contestant stepped out of the arena, Luke spotted the next rider. "Look over there. Here comes the next competitor."

"It's a girl! They do this, too?"

"Of course. Didn't you know that girls, including your sisters, can do anything boys can do?"

"That's what they keep telling me. Especially Tilly. It's tough being the only guy in the house sometimes."

Luke noticed there was a slight delay before the next ride. Now was a good time to see if Tucker would open up a little more to him. "I guess it would be. Have you ever tried to talk to your aunt Meg about it?"

"But she's a girl, too. She wouldn't understand."

"I wouldn't be so sure. I grew up with your aunt. She was one of my best friends."

"I didn't know girls could be a best friend." Tucker scratched his head.

"Sure. Your aunt was always a great listener. Whenever I had a problem, I'd go to her first."

"Didn't you have any brothers or sisters to talk to?"

"I have three brothers. They're all older than me, so they weren't around much. I guess they didn't want to be bothered by their baby brother." Luke had always hoped at least one of his brothers would take the time to maybe take him fishing or teach him how to ride a bike. "I think it's pretty cool you and your sisters are all the same age. You can experience new things at the same time."

"Yeah, I guess so."

"You might not think so now, but when you get older, you'll appreciate it." Luke noticed the little girl who had been inside the chute earlier had returned. "I think she's ready to go." Luke pointed.

The door flung open, and the sheep tore out across the arena. The crowd roared as the child hung on tight.

"She's going longer than the boy did!" Tucker jumped to his feet. His laughter filled Luke's heart with joy.

"Look at her go. Hold on!" Luke cheered.

Seconds later, the crowd erupted in hoots and hollers when the girl took a gentle tumble to the ground.

"Does that mean that she wins?" Tucker questioned.

The girl ran around the rink smiling while doing fist pumps and waving to her fans.

"She has the best score so far, but we have a lot more riders to watch." Luke eyed his watch and wished he could spend the entire afternoon alone with Tucker.

"Really? There's more?" Tucker bounced up and down in his seat.

"Yes." Luke reached inside his back pocket and removed the pamphlet he had picked up earlier. "According to the lineup, there's going to be fifteen competitors. There's another group scheduled for later in the afternoon, too."

"Can we stay and watch them all?"

Luke couldn't be late to meet Meg. "We might not be able to watch everyone in this first session, but we have plenty of time before we have to meet your aunt and the girls for lunch."

"Can I go down there and ride? I'm sure I can hold on a lot longer than the other kids."

This hadn't been part of the plan. Yes, he did want to have a breakthrough with Tucker, to bring a little joy back into the boy's life, but his desire to sign up to ride wasn't a good thing. It was exactly what Meg feared. "Sorry, buddy. All the children's parents registered them in advance. So you won't be able to ride today."

"But what about the next time? Maybe we can find out when there'll be another rodeo like this. I'll ask Aunt Meg to find out."

Luke's stomach twisted. "I don't think that's a good idea. At least not for now. Why don't you keep that between you and me? Maybe I can work on it." Luke could feel beads of perspiration forming on his forehead.

"You would do that for me?"

"Sure. I'll see what I can do, but remember not to say anything today to your aunt or your sisters."

Tucker flashed a wide grin. "I won't. I promise not to say a word. It will be just between us guys. Thank you for bringing me here today. I haven't had this much fun since my daddy took me camping."

Luke's heart squeezed. It would have been nice if his father had taken him camping. Or at least shown any interest in spending time with his youngest son. Luke shook off the negative thoughts. That was water under the bridge. Today was about Tucker and bringing some happiness back into his life. He wouldn't allow his father to ruin the day.

An hour later, countless sheep had torn across the arena with children holding on as tight as they could. Luke checked his watch. It was time for him and Tucker to head to the food court to meet up with Meg and the girls.

Tucker hung close to Luke, skipping and rehashing the entire event from start to finish. "I can't wait for Tilly and Tia to watch the mutton busting live. I know Tilly, she'll want to try it, too. But Tia would probably rather just watch."

"I think you're right. Tilly seems quite brave."

"Yeah, she's not afraid to try anything. I don't think Aunt Meg likes it much." Tucker snickered.

Luke had a feeling Meg wasn't going to like Tucker's sudden interest in mutton busting. She'd be relieved to see him happy and having a good time, but she wasn't going to like the reason.

She knew the allure of the cowboy lifestyle for young boys. Luke had been drawn to the life, especially once it made him feel loved by his parents. When he'd gotten older and was competing every weekend, the glamour soon faded. He'd realized that he could never win enough to make his parents love him for just being him and not for being a champion bull rider. But by then he was addicted to the thrill of winning and the stability he believed it provided.

Across the room, he spotted Meg and the girls sitting at a round table. He sucked in a breath, sent up a silent prayer for Tucker and prepared himself for the fallout.

Chapter Seven

"Aunt Meg! Aunt Meg!" Tucker sprinted toward the table like a startled deer crossing a busy highway.

Her heart exploded with joy. She had to do a double take to make sure it was him. Curly hair. Check. Freckled face. Check. But his expression was something unfamiliar.

She rose and wrapped her arms around her stomach. Tears of happiness brimmed her lashes. This was the first time since she'd moved back to Whispering Slopes and stepped into the role of mother to her sister's children that she'd seen Tucker this happy. The kid was beaming. He looked like a different child.

Tucker grabbed his aunt around her waist and hugged her tight. "I had the best time ever! You have to come see it. Mutton busting is awesome!" He squeezed even harder.

"Yeah, let's go watch, Aunt Meg. Please!" Tilly was the first to react to Tucker's enthusiasm.

Meg's emotions were mixed. She was thrilled to see Tucker over the moon about something. The past year he'd shown no excitement about anything. Being exposed to new things was one of the best things about being a child. That's what her head was telling her, but her heart was feeling something different. Why did something that caused her so much pain have to be the catalyst to bringing Tucker back to life?

"Let's get some lunch before we decide what we're going to do next." Luke's gaze settled on Meg. "Smell that delicious aroma. There's nothing better than unhealthy rodeo food." He laughed.

"We can eat anytime. I want to go see the sheep. Maybe I can ride one, too." Tilly looked back and forth between the adults. "I know I can hang on longer than those kids in the video."

"Mr. Luke is right. We all need a good lunch first." Meg glanced down at Tucker and smiled. "I'm so happy you had a good time. I can't wait to hear all about it." But did she want to? His excitement mirrored Luke's enthusiasm from childhood. After his uncle had taken him to the rodeo for the first time, he'd come knocking on her door so thrilled he could hardly speak.

"Oh, man. I can't wait to be an adult so I can make my own decisions." Tilly put her elbows on the table and frowned.

Meg remembered feeling the same way as Tilly at that age. Boy, had she ever been wrong. Being an adult wasn't for the faint of heart.

"Why don't I go and place our order? Are cheeseburgers, fries and chocolate milkshakes good for everyone?" Luke scanned the table.

Meg answered first. "Sounds good to me. Kids, is that what you'd like?"

The children all cheered yes. Luke turned to go and put in the order. Tilly sprang from her seat. "I'll go with you, Cowboy Luke!"

Meg considered Tilly. The child looked up at Luke

with an expression she knew all too well. She remembered looking up to her father the very same way. He'd been her world. The only thing she had ever wanted was his time.

"After lunch, can we go back and watch the afternoon session of mutton busting?"

Tucker's question pulled Meg from thoughts about her father.

"Can we—please?" Tia spoke for the first time. Great. Now she was on the bandwagon. It was one against four. Although Luke hadn't said one way or another, Meg knew where he stood. There was no way she could say no and disappoint the children, especially Tucker. "Sure. We can go."

"Yes!" Tucker did a fist pump and jumped up from the table. "I'm going to go tell Cowboy Luke that you said yes. Thank you." He gave her another quick hug.

Meg didn't have a chance to respond before Tucker was gone. She needed to put the thoughts about her father out of her mind and be thankful for Tucker's smile, no matter the reason behind it.

"Aunt Meg, don't forget we need three dozen cupcakes for school tomorrow," Tilly announced as she skipped into the kitchen early Monday morning.

The start of a new week and she was already behind. Thankfully, Miss Mattie had gotten the kids their breakfast this morning. Meg exhaled a slow and steady breath. "Why didn't you mention this sooner? The last time this happened, I told you I needed a little more notice."

"I did tell you. Remember…I gave you the flyer."

Meg moved toward the kitchen counter and reached for Tilly's sparkly pink backpack. She opened the zipper and pulled out her math and history books, a handful of wrappers and pieces of chewed gum. "Have you been chewing gum in class?"

Tilly's gaze moved to the floor. "I was chewing it on the school bus, but once I got into the classroom, I forgot I had it in my mouth, so I stuck it in my bag."

Meg rolled her eyes. "You shouldn't be chewing gum on the bus, either. We need to start working on your organizational skills. Your book bag is a disaster."

"I like it messy."

Meg had to bite her tongue to keep from laughing. Tilly reminded her so much of her sister at that age. Headstrong and fearless.

Meg scanned through the stack of papers. Among the pages was a letter dated two weeks ago. It was from the children's school asking parents to contribute a baked good to their annual fundraiser. Meg looked up from the paper. "You've known about the bake sale for fourteen days and you're just now telling me?"

"I'm sorry." Her lower lip rolled. "Tia and I can help you bake after school today."

Meg's heart softened. How could she stay angry at that sweet face? Tilly hadn't done this on purpose. "That would be nice of you and your sister."

"I'll ask Cowboy Luke if he wants to help, too!"

Meg laughed, picturing Luke filling cupcake tins with batter. "I think he's got enough to do with the repairs on the B&B. Let's get your things back into your bag. The bus will be here in a couple of minutes. Are your sister and brother ready?"

"Tia is reading, but she's dressed and ready to go."

"What about Tucker?"

"He's in his room pretending to ride a sheep. He wanted to get on my back and have me try and throw him off." Tilly rolled her eyes.

Since they had attended the rodeo on Saturday, Tucker had talked nonstop about wanting Meg to buy some sheep. Her emotions had been too jumbled to share any of this with Luke.

"Well, run upstairs and tell them to come down with their backpacks." She probably needed to go through theirs to see if there were any more surprises.

"Okay." Tilly dashed from the kitchen and thundered up the steps.

The sounds of silverware clinking carried in from the dining room. Miss Mattie had served Luke his breakfast about twenty minutes ago, so he was probably finishing up. Last week Joe showed up around eight o'clock each morning to help Luke with the repairs.

Miss Mattie scurried into the room carrying a plate with silverware stacked on top. "Mr. Beckett has had his breakfast. I'm going to top off his coffee before I head upstairs to take care of his room. Do you need help with the children?"

Meg had wanted to speak with Luke and now was as good a time as ever. "No, I'm good, thanks. I'll get the coffee. You go ahead and do what you have to do upstairs. Once Joe arrives to help Luke, I'll check with him to see if he'd like breakfast this morning."

"That's nice of you, dear. There's plenty left since the children hardly ate anything."

"What about Tucker? Did he eat?" Last night at dinner, he'd barely eaten a bite.

"Hardly." She laughed. "Between each bite, he went on and on about riding sheep. It's nice to see him smiling again."

Meg agreed. Tucker was like a different child. "Well, hopefully he won't come downstairs complaining of his stomach." But she didn't think this morning would be any different. According to her sister, Tucker had complained of stomach ailments each morning after his father left their family. Once his mother was gone, the complaints sometimes persisted throughout the day. "I'll slip a banana in his lunch box in case he gets hungry."

Miss Mattie nodded. "That's a good idea." She turned and headed upstairs.

Meg grabbed the pot of coffee and took it to the dining room.

Luke looked up from the newspaper spread out on the table. "Good morning." He smiled.

"Good morning to you. I have hot coffee for you." She filled the cup, picked up another for herself and poured. "Do you mind if I join you for a few minutes?"

Luke closed the paper, folded it twice and set it on the chair next to him. "I'd like that."

Meg gripped her hands tight around the cup and sipped the coffee. She pulled out the chair and took a seat across from Luke. "I guess you're waiting on Joe?" She'd never been good at small talk, but discussing her feelings about rodeo life had never been easy, either.

"Yeah, he should be here anytime. I hope to get the drywall finished today in the hawk's nest suite."

"How's your neck?" Meg had been afraid Luke might be overdoing it. He and Joe had worked long hours last week.

Luke rubbed his hand up and down his neck. "It's feeling pretty good. I've been doing the exercises. I think our last session together helped. I guess you know what you're doing," he joked.

In a perfect world, Meg would be treating her patients full-time. She felt a great sense of accomplishment from the job. Discovering the patient's individual goal and incorporating those goals into a rehabilitation plan that worked best for their particular situation was a priority. But she couldn't go back on the promise she'd made to Gina to keep the B&B open. Her sister believed closing would be too much change at once for her children. If only she'd thought through the ramifications of abandoning her children.

"Well, I hope I do. It's what I love. There's something rewarding about helping someone who is in pain."

"I know you mentioned your promise to Gina, but do you think there will be a time when you'll ever have full-time hours? I'm sure the town is full of people with a lot of aches and pains." Luke laughed.

"There definitely wouldn't be a lack of business if I were to expand my hours. Unfortunately, between the children and the B&B, it's just not possible right now. Maybe when they go off to college…"

She forced a smile. A future without the kids around sounded lonely to Meg. She hoped that they would keep in touch once they grew up and had lives of their own, but who knew. Meg gazed out through the French doors.

"What's up? I can tell there's something on your mind."

She smiled. "It's nice to know some things don't change. You always could tell when something was bothering me."

Luke extended his hand across the table. "I know having me here is awkward for you. It is for me, too, but whatever happened in our past, I hope you still consider me a friend. And someone you can talk to."

Their eyes remained fixated on one another until Meg broke the stare. "I haven't had an opportunity to thank you for what you did with Tucker."

"That's not necessary. We had a lot of fun together."

"At the rodeo on Saturday, it was the first time I'd seen Tucker smile since I came to care for him and his sisters. The day I arrived in Whispering Slopes, he wouldn't come out of his room. For weeks, he wouldn't talk to me or even look at me. I think he thought my presence meant his parents would never return. Of course, I knew my sister—she wasn't coming back." Meg shrugged her shoulders.

Luke remained silent and listened.

"The first couple of months after Gina left, I tried to keep the kids in the routine they'd been used to. The girls slowly adjusted to a new normal, but Tucker never wanted any part of me trying to make a life for him and his sisters. To watch him go month after month with no joy has been heartbreaking. So, what you've done is a big deal. A huge deal. I don't think I'll ever forget the look on his face when I saw him running to the table at the food court."

Meg wiped a stray tear. Something good had emerged from the rodeo experience. "I knew my prayers had been answered. You'd gotten through to him… something I hadn't been able to do. I just wanted you to know how much that meant to me."

Meg watched Luke as he ran his index finger along the rim of his coffee cup. "I was glad to help. Tucker and I have a lot in common."

Footsteps thundered down the staircase. Tucker ran into the dining room with his backpack flung over his shoulder. Meg braced herself for another round of "I have a stomachache. I don't want to go to school." She was caught off guard when she was met with a smile.

Tucker turned his attention to Luke. "Maybe when I

get home from school, if you've finished working, we can do something."

Meg waited for Luke's response. He probably had other things to do once he finished working on the room.

"That sounds like a good idea, buddy." Luke took a sip of his coffee and placed the cup back on the table. "I'll probably need to head into town to pick up a few things at the hardware store. Maybe you can come with me—if it's okay with your aunt Meg."

"That would be awesome!" Tucker bounced up and down as he turned to Meg. "Can I—please?"

"I don't see why not. But how is your stomach? Are you feeling okay this morning?" Meg asked despite Tucker acting like he was fine.

"I feel grrreat!"

Outside, the school bus tooted its horn.

The girls dashed down the steps and out the screen door. "Bye, Aunt Meg," the two yelled in unison.

Tucker leaned over and kissed Meg on the cheek. "See you later," he called out as he followed his sisters out the door.

Meg couldn't deny how happy she was to see Tucker enthusiastic and happy. Maybe she'd overreacted about exposing him to the rodeo. So far, he hadn't asked to go again. That was a good sign. Sure, he talked a lot about the day, but what little boy wouldn't be excited by a day at the rodeo?

Meg was grateful to Luke, but as she watched him looking out the window at the children, she wondered why Luke felt he and Tucker had so much in common.

After Meg left the dining room, Luke remained at the table sipping his coffee. Seeing Tucker so happy before heading off to school had made his morning. Now if he could only get up the courage to talk to Meg about his promise to Tucker. Last night he had searched online and found a farm in Lexington that operated a day camp for children. The camp wasn't permanent—it moved around almost like a carnival. Its goal was to expose children to life on a farm and to get them interested in the rodeo. When he'd read that they offered mutton busting, he had to restrain himself from signing up. He couldn't do that without Meg's permission.

Dishes rattled in the kitchen. He pushed himself away from the table and picked up his coffee cup. No time like the present. He snatched the newspaper and stuck it under his arm. Luke peeked around the corner and spotted Meg at the kitchen sink, gazing out the window. He stayed at the door so he wouldn't startle her. "Do you need some help with the dishes?"

Meg turned. "I usually don't put my guests to work." She smiled. "Besides, you're doing enough work already with the remodeling."

Luke laughed. "I'm just killing time waiting for Joe." He moved over toward the sink and set his paper on the island.

Meg continued to rinse the breakfast dishes. "If you'd like, you can load those into the dishwasher." She nodded toward the stack of plates on the counter.

"I'm on it." One by one he placed dishes on the rack. "I guess you're a little relieved Tucker didn't put up a fight about going to school and complain about a stomachache."

"Yes, it's a huge relief—thanks to you. I also appreciate your offer to do something with him after school today. You're the reason he left with a smile on his face."

"Well, I hope you'll keep that in mind when you consider my question." He couldn't ignore the way Meg's body stiffened when she turned to face him. Getting her on board would be a challenge, but he had to try.

"Does this have to do with mutton busting?" Her left brow arched.

Luke couldn't get Tucker's smiling face out of his mind. "I kind of made a promise to Tucker. Maybe it was wrong, but I can't go back on my word. He doesn't trust adults as it is."

Meg turned off the faucet, leaned her back against the countertop and crossed her arms. "I'm listening."

"On Saturday, I wish you could've seen Tucker's re-action when the first child came out of the chute at the mutton busting competition. I know you saw his excite-ment at the food court, but just imagine it amplified. I remember feeling the same way. I can't even explain it."

"I remember. When you came to my house after your uncle took you to your first competition, I'd never seen you act that way before. I knew the rodeo would always be a part of your life. I don't want that life for Tucker. I thought I'd made it clear."

"I know you don't, but I think not giving him the opportunity could do more harm."

"What exactly did you promise him?"

Luke swallowed the lump in his throat. "I told him I would talk to you and ask your permission to let him at least try the sport." He paused for a reaction, but she remained quiet. "There's a chance he could enjoy watch-ing it more than actually doing it. You know how kids can be. They lose interest quickly."

"But what if he doesn't?"

"I suppose we'll deal with that when the time comes." Luke realized it was a risk.

"I think you're mistaken. You'll be back on tour,

and I'll be the one left to handle the situation. I know my sister would not want any of her children joining the rodeo. Growing up, she felt the same way as I did about our father's profession. It robbed us of a normal family life."

"I know you don't want Tucker to grow up and run off to join the rodeo circuit. I completely understand. But we need to get him through this challenging time in his life. I honestly believe this will help him work through his abandonment issues." Getting involved with the rodeo at a young age had helped Luke to feel better about himself. It had saved his life. He'd developed a stronger sense of confidence, even if it hadn't changed his relationship with his parents. Sure, they showed more interest when he started to win, but he remained the "surprise" baby who had never been wanted.

"What exactly did you have in mind?"

Over the next couple of minutes, Luke explained the camp he'd found online. He had to give her credit for listening to his argument.

"I suppose the one plus is even if he does get hooked on the camp, it's not permanent and it will move on. Maybe by the time it comes around again, he'll be interested in something else."

"I'm glad you're thinking that way. And don't forget, it won't interfere with school since it's only on Saturday mornings—another plus." He was hesitant to ask, but if she gave him the okay, he needed to get Tucker registered soon. "So, does this mean you're giving me the green light? I won't say anything to Tucker about the camp unless I have your permission."

Meg stared at the floor and then looked up with a nod. "Against my better judgment, you have my permission. Just don't let him get hurt."

"I promise. You're doing the right thing, Meg. This will be a good experience for Tucker."

Meg's consent sent adrenaline surging through Luke's body. He was determined to rid Tucker of the negative mindset instilled by his parents' bad decisions. If he wasn't successful, those wounds would fester inside Tucker's mind for a lifetime, as they had for Luke. No. He wouldn't allow it. Luke exhaled a slow and steady breath. He couldn't wait to share the news with Tucker.

Chapter Eight

Meg locked the door of her office and slid her sunglasses over her eyes to shield them from the glare of the late afternoon sun. She'd had a busy day with patients, even forgoing the Thursday turkey sandwich special at Buser's General. She strolled down the sidewalk toward the post office. Her stomach grumbled. The day had been jam-packed with patients, and she'd never been happier. Luke had been one of the patients on her calendar. She was pleased to see he was making good progress, and the mobility in his neck was improving. He'd been diligently doing the exercises she had prescribed, to which he attributed his continued healing.

Meg rounded the corner and spotted Tucker's teacher approaching. "Good afternoon, Mrs. Cooper." The last time they had spoken was in the principal's office. Thankfully since that day, Tucker hadn't been in any more fights.

"Hello, Meg. I'm glad I bumped into you. I had planned to give you a call later today." She plopped her leather tote on the sidewalk and rubbed her right arm.

"Are you having problems with your shoulder?" Meg

was used to people coming up to her on the street with a list of their aches and pains.

"Nothing that removing some items from my over-stuffed bag wouldn't cure." She laughed.

Meg's lighthearted mood from a productive day began to fade. Had Tucker been in another fight? "I hope there isn't anything wrong. You're not having problems again with Tucker, are you?"

The elderly woman smiled and shook her head. "Oh, no. Not in the least. The past couple of days he seems to be more like his sweet little self. That's what I wanted to talk to you about."

Meg released a breath and prepared herself. "What's going on?"

"I wanted to let you know how thrilled I am that Tucker has been making more of an effort to get along with the other children. He's been a dream student this week. I understand Luke Beckett is the reason behind this change."

Meg had managed to get through Luke's therapy session without discussing Tucker or the mutton busting camp. If she didn't talk about it, maybe it would just go away. Maybe magically Tucker would lose interest. That proved to be wishful thinking. Since Luke had told Tucker their plans for this Saturday, he had talked nonstop about it. She kept reminding herself it was only a two-week camp. Then in just a few short weeks, Luke would be gone and out of her life permanently. Hopefully once he left Whispering Slopes, he would take with him any desire Tucker might have to join the rodeo. "What has Tucker said to you?"

"Not just to me, to the entire class. He's come out of his shell."

Meg was happy for Tucker, but she still had her concerns. "That's great to hear."

"He's introduced the entire class to mutton busting. I must say, he has me curious, as well. He even demonstrated with Tilly climbing on his back. The children loved it. That's why I wanted to talk with you."

"I hope he's not disrupting your classroom and preventing you from getting through your lessons." Tonight, she'd talk with Tucker. He needed to leave mutton busting out of the classroom.

"Oh, no, not in the least. I thought since the children are so curious about riding sheep and the rodeo in general, maybe Luke could come and speak to the children."

Meg considered the teacher's suggestion. "Do you think that's a good idea? There might be some parents who would rather their children not be bitten by the rodeo bug." She was one of those parents, but unfortunately, it might be too late.

"I can't imagine the parents would have a problem. Most are big rodeo fans themselves. But I did plan on blasting out an email to make sure there are no objections."

"You're right about Whispering Slopes having a lot of rodeo enthusiasts." But how many had been raised by a famous bull rider father? None that she knew. They could never understand what it had been like for her growing up and trying to compete for her father's attention. Another reason for her to get Luke healed and back on the road. She didn't need a constant reminder of the pain.

"Before I reach out to the parents, I wanted to know if you would run this by Luke to see if he'd be interested. Tucker seemed to think Luke would say yes if you were the one to ask him. I suppose he thinks Luke still has a soft spot in his heart for you. But since you two are spending so much time together, I thought you wouldn't mind asking him."

"Luke is a guest at my B&B—nothing more."

Mrs. Cooper chuckled. "Not according to Tilly and Tia."

Meg's face warmed. Oh, no. What exactly had the girls been telling their teacher?

Mrs. Cooper gently rested her hand on Meg's arm. "Oh dear, don't be embarrassed. We all know you and Luke used to be high school sweethearts."

We all? Who were the children talking to? Meg's stomach flipped. "I'm not sure what the girls have said to you, but Luke and I are just friends." Did the woman believe her? Judging from the sly smile on her face, Meg wasn't so sure.

"I overheard the girls telling a couple of the children that you and Luke were getting married."

For a second, Meg's ears lost all their ability to hear. What in the world? Why would they think this? She hadn't done anything that would lead them to believe there was any future for her and Luke. "I'm sorry, but the girls are mistaken. Luke will be returning to Colorado. His life is with the rodeo. Not here in Whispering Slopes." He'd made his choice.

"I guess the girls were mistaken. I'm sorry if I embarrassed you. I was just going by what I heard."

Meg could only imagine how many of the children had spread the rumor to their parents.

She recalled her earlier appointment with the mayor. He had asked her about Luke. The man kept going on about how good it was to have him back in town. He'd even winked at Meg when she mentioned Luke would be returning to Colorado. Judging by his actions, he must've heard the rumor, too. Meg shook her head. When she got home, the first thing she planned to do was to have a long talk with all the children. She had to put an end to their spreading false rumors.

"I'll admit, I was rather excited by the thought of you and Luke reuniting and getting married. I was picturing a beautiful ceremony at your B&B. It would be the perfect venue. Your love story is much like the romance novels that I enjoy reading on occasion." She laughed.

Meg's stomach squeezed. "Well, I'm sorry to disappoint you, but Luke and I have no future together. I hope if you hear otherwise from anyone in town, you'll clarify the situation."

"Of course. Do you think you could still ask Luke about speaking to the class? I know the children would love it."

Luke was trying to keep a low profile while in town. This might not be something he would want to do. Then again, he seemed to love children. "I can ask, but he's been busy. He's helping me with the repairs on the B&B."

Mrs. Cooper clasped her hands together. "That's certainly nice of him. I always thought he was a good young man. If you could just run it by him, I'd appreciate it. He can give me a call if he has any questions. I better run. It was good seeing you, dear." She picked up her tote bag and flung it over her shoulder.

Meg stood frozen, watching Mrs. Cooper scurry off down the sidewalk. Married. She couldn't believe Tilly and Tia would make up such a thing.

Meg made her way toward the post office. Once inside she walked toward the back wall, where her post office box was located. Her key was barely inside the lock when she heard a squeal and the sound of high heels clicking on the tile floor.

"I can't believe you didn't call and tell me!"

Meg turned as her old high school friend Cindy Graham flung her arm around Meg's neck. "I'm so excited for you!" She released her viselike grip.

"What's going on?" The second she asked, Meg realized what Cindy was referring to. The small-town rumor mill was in overdrive. Word was spreading like peanut butter on warm toast.

"Oh, you're so silly." Cindy batted her hand and giggled. "You and Luke getting married! I always knew the two of you would get back together. If anyone should be a couple, it's you and Luke Beckett. When's the wedding? Are you going to get married in Whispering Slopes? Will you have to sell the B&B and move to Colorado? I heard that's where he lives. I've followed his career from the beginning. Now don't get mad, but I had a little crush on Luke back in high school, but no one had a chance up against you."

Meg's head was spinning. It was obvious she wasn't going to get a word in until Cindy got through her list of questions. And she wasn't showing any sign of coming up for air, so Meg waited.

"Tell me all the details. Will you have the ceremony at the B&B? It's the perfect spot." Cindy clapped her hands together like her former self as the captain of their high school cheerleading squad.

The B&B—that seemed to be the consensus around town. "I hate to squash your enthusiasm, but there's not going to be a wedding."

Cindy's smooth forehead wrinkled before her face ignited with a smile. "Oh, you're going to elope. That's so romantic. Are you going to escape to a tropical island and get married on the beach in your bare feet? I always thought I'd like to do that… Of course, I have to find a man first." She giggled like a teenager. "You know what it's like to live in a small town. It doesn't provide us single girls with too many options. You're blessed that your old boyfriend came back for you."

This had to stop. "Hold up, Cindy." Meg placed her hand in the air.

"What is it?"

Meg inhaled a slow and steady breath, then released. "First of all, Luke did not come back to town for me. He simply came for a little relaxation." Since his return, Luke had shown little remorse over his sudden departure that had left her heartbroken.

"But—"

"Let me finish. Second, there is no elopement or wedding—we haven't reunited. I'm not sure where you got your information, but it's false."

Cindy placed her hand on her cheek. "Let's see…I think I overheard it when I was in the produce section. Lindsay Patterson was talking to someone on her cell phone. You know how she likes to talk loud."

This was worse than Meg could ever have imagined. Since their high school days, Lindsay had always been the biggest gossip. If you wanted anything to be kept a secret, you certainly couldn't tell her. "I'm not sure where Lindsay might have heard such an outlandish story, but there's no truth to it."

"I'm sorry, Meg. Please don't be mad. I thought the news was true. Our entire graduating class always believed you and Luke would get married and raise a big family."

Meg had thought the same right up until Luke left the day after graduation. "I'm not mad. I just wish people would check the facts before spreading the news all over town."

Cindy reached for Meg's hand. "I'll give Lindsay a call and tell her to zip it."

Meg smiled. "I would appreciate that."

"I better run." Cindy gave Meg a quick hug. "You okay?"

"Sure—I'm fine. I'll see you later." Meg turned around to retrieve her mail from the post office box. Tilly and Tia had been wrong to make up such a story, but she really couldn't blame them. They missed their father and mother. The family they once were. But she'd have to make it clear there was no way she would allow Luke to become a permanent part of her life. He'd broken her heart once, and she wouldn't allow that to happen a second time. But would telling them break their hearts again?

"It looks like you might need to add some oil." Luke pulled the dipstick from Joe's old pickup truck. Gravel crunched in the distance. He glanced up from the greasy engine and spotted Meg's SUV traveling down the driveway at a hurried speed. A cloud of dust rode her tail.

Luke closed the hood on the vehicle and dusted off his hands. "Thanks again for your help on the room today. It's a good thing you spotted the wiring issue."

"No problem. Do you want me to hang around while you break the bad news to Meg?"

Luke shook his head. "Thanks, but I'll take care of it." The issue would create a delay, but it was a blessing that the problem was discovered.

"Sounds good." Joe extended his hand. "I'll call Connor and give him a heads-up."

"Thanks, buddy. I'll let you know the plan once I speak with Meg."

Joe climbed inside his truck. He offered a wave to Meg as she parked her car and exited. She circled to the trunk.

Luke approached. "Do you need any help?"

She pushed up the sleeves of her sweater. "That would be great. I had to stop at the market on the way home. Do you know if the children are inside?"

"No, they all went down to the barn. Tucker wanted to use them to practice mutton busting. Tilly seems to be under the impression that if she helps Tucker, she'll get to come along to the camp. She's determined to show everyone that girls can ride sheep just the same as boys." Luke laughed, but Meg's expression told him she wasn't in a laughing mood. "Is something wrong?" Luke grabbed the two reusable shopping bags filled with groceries and closed the trunk.

Meg rolled her eyes. "I need to talk to you about something, but let's get the groceries into the house. There's chicken I need to get into the refrigerator."

Inside the kitchen, Luke placed the bags on top of the counter and started to unpack the groceries. Meg removed the chicken from the bag and placed it in the refrigerator. She turned abruptly and raked her fingers through her hair. "The girls have been making up stories." Her face flushed.

"Oh yeah? That's nice. Is this something for school? I wouldn't mind hearing them."

Meg frowned. "No. This isn't a story you want to hear. Trust me. They're telling their friends at school that you and I are getting married."

Luke laughed. Oh boy. No wonder Meg looked so mad.

"It's not funny. They've told a couple of their friends, and now it's all over town."

"Calm down. Maybe it's not that bad."

Meg placed the jug of orange juice in the refrigerator and whirled around. "Oh, yes, it is. Even Lindsay Patterson knows. She's telling everyone who will listen. You know how she is—Lindsay lives to spread gossip."

Luke remembered Lindsay well. She was like the town crier. "I guess there's not much we can do."

"Of course there is. I've got to nip this in the bud. The first thing I'm going to do is have a long talk with all three of the children. I might have to punish them. Maybe no TV for the next week."

"Come on, it's not that big of a deal." Luke smiled.

"Maybe not for you, but it is for me. You don't live here. Who knows, by now the entire town probably thinks we're getting married." She placed both hands on her hips. "And stop smiling. You need to take this more seriously."

Luke bit the inside of his mouth to keep from laughing. Meg's face was turning redder by the minute. He'd forgotten how cute she could be when she got angry at him. "At this point, the damage has been done. There's not much we can do, so let's try and forget about it."

Meg placed the last of the dry goods in the pantry. "I need to go find the kids before they tell the story to anyone else."

There was no stopping her. "Try and go easy on them. I'm sure they didn't mean any harm. Considering what they've gone through, I can't say I blame them."

Meg's expression softened. "I know you're right, but they need to understand they can't make up stories like this and share them with others. It's one thing for them to imagine something like that between themselves, but it's wrong to spread it all over town."

Luke considered the situation. Could Meg ever imag-

ine a life with him? Probably not after he'd left her high
and dry, but he'd explained all that in the letter, yet
she'd never reached out to him. Not even a phone call.
He could only conclude that his words didn't matter to
her. Maybe she'd never loved him after all. The best
thing he could do was to continue to focus on getting
well and returning to Colorado so he could continue to
compete and win.

"Before you go and have your talk, there's something
I need to speak with you about."

Luke removed the box of pasta and folded the empty
canvas grocery bag.

"I'm not sure I like the tone in your voice. Is there
something wrong?"

"There's a bit of a problem with the hawk's nest suite.
But don't panic. We'll get it taken care of."

Meg approached the island and brushed her hand on
top of the granite. "What's up?"

"It's the wiring on the back wall, next to the bathroom. Joe and I pulled out the drywall earlier. Unfortunately, we discovered a lot of the wires appear to be
frayed."

Meg blew out a breath. "How could that happen?"

"More than likely it was caused by some kind of ro-
dent. Probably mice. It can happen in older homes, but
it is something that needs to be addressed since it's a
fire hazard."

Meg's shoulders slumped. "This sounds like a costly
problem."

"It shouldn't be too bad if the damage is just confined to that room. The other walls in the suite appear
to be in good shape, but we haven't removed any of the
drywall in the eagle's nest."

Meg remained silent, digesting the unsettling news.

Loyal Readers
FREE BOOKS Voucher

We're giving away THOUSANDS of FREE BOOKS

Romance

Suspense

Don't Miss Out! Send for Your Free Books Today!

Get up to 4
FREE FABULOUS BOOKS
You Love!

To thank you for being a loyal reader we'd like to send you up to 4 FREE BOOKS, absolutely free.

Just write "YES" on the Loyal Reader Voucher and we'll send you up to 4 Free Books and Free Mystery Gifts, altogether worth over $20, as a way of saying thank you for being a loyal reader.

Try **Love Inspired® Romance Larger-Print** books and fall in love with inspirational romances that take you on an uplifting journey of faith, forgiveness and hope.

Try **Love Inspired® Suspense Larger-Print** books where courage and optimism unite in stories of faith and love in the face of danger.

Or **TRY BOTH!**

We are so glad you love the books as much as we do and can't wait to send you great new books.

So don't miss out, return your Loyal Reader Voucher Today!

Pam Powers

LOYAL READER
FREE BOOKS VOUCHER

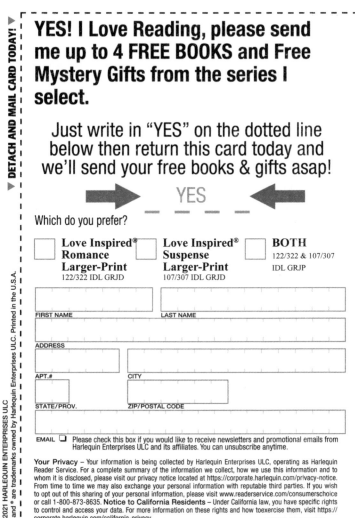

► DETACH AND MAIL CARD TODAY! ▼

YES! I Love Reading, please send me up to 4 FREE BOOKS and Free Mystery Gifts from the series I select.

Just write in "YES" on the dotted line below then return this card today and we'll send your free books & gifts asap!

➡ YES ⬅

Which do you prefer?

☐ **Love Inspired®**
Romance
Larger-Print
122/322 IDL GRJD

☐ **Love Inspired®**
Suspense
Larger-Print
107/307 IDL GRJD

☐ **BOTH**
122/322 & 107/307
IDL GRJP

FIRST NAME

LAST NAME

ADDRESS

APT.#

CITY

STATE/PROV.

ZIP/POSTAL CODE

EMAIL ☐ Please check this box if you would like to receive newsletters and promotional emails from Harlequin Enterprises ULC and its affiliates. You can unsubscribe anytime.

Your Privacy – Your information is being collected by Harlequin Enterprises ULC, operating as Harlequin Reader Service. For a complete summary of the information we collect, how we use this information and to whom it is disclosed, please visit our privacy notice located at https://corporate.harlequin.com/privacy-notice. From time to time we may also exchange your personal information with reputable third parties. If you wish to opt out of this sharing of your personal information, please visit www.readerservice.com/consumerschoice or call 1-800-873-8635. **Notice to California Residents** – Under California law, you have specific rights to control and access your data. For more information on these rights and how to exercise them, visit https://corporate.harlequin.com/california-privacy.

© 2021 HARLEQUIN ENTERPRISES ULC
™ and ® are trademarks owned by Harlequin Enterprises ULC. Printed in the U.S.A.

LI/SLI-520-LR21

◆HARLEQUIN Reader Service — **Here's how it works:**

Accepting your 2 free books and 2 free gifts (gifts valued at approximately $10.00 retail) places you under no obligation to buy anything. You may keep the books and gifts and return the shipping statement marked "cancel." If you do not cancel, approximately one month later we'll send you 6 more books from each series you have chosen, and bill you at our low, subscribers-only discount price. Love Inspired® Romance Larger-Print books and Love Inspired® Suspense Larger-Print books consist of 6 books each month and cost just $5.99 each in the U.S. or $6.24 each in Canada. That is a savings of at least 17% off the cover price. It's quite a bargain! Shipping and handling is just 50¢ per book in the U.S. and $1.25 per book in Canada*. You may return any shipment at our expense and cancel at any time — or you may continue to receive monthly shipments at our low, subscribers-only discount price plus shipping and handling. *Terms and prices subject to change without notice. Prices do not include sales taxes which will be charged (if applicable) based on your state or country of residence. Canadian residents will be charged applicable taxes. Offer not valid in Quebec. Books received may not be as shown. All orders subject to approval. Credit or debit balances in a customer's account(s) may be offset by any other outstanding balance owed by or to the customer. Please allow 3 to 4 weeks for delivery. Offer available while quantities last. **Your Privacy** – Your information is being collected by Harlequin Enterprises ULC, operating as Harlequin Reader Service. For a complete summary of the information we collect, how we use this information and to whom it is disclosed, please visit our privacy notice located at https://corporate.harlequin.com/privacy-notice. From time to time we may also exchange your personal information with reputable third parties. If you wish to opt out of this sharing of your personal information, please visit www.readerservice.com/consumerschoice or call 1-800-873-8635. **Notice to California Residents** – Under California law, you have specific rights to control and access your data. For more information on these rights and how to exercise them, visit https://corporate.harlequin.com/california-privacy.

▲ If offer card is missing write to: Harlequin Reader Service, P.O. Box 1341, Buffalo, NY 14240-8531 or visit www.ReaderService.com ▲

BUSINESS REPLY MAIL
FIRST-CLASS MAIL   PERMIT NO. 717   BUFFALO, NY

POSTAGE WILL BE PAID BY ADDRESSEE

HARLEQUIN READER SERVICE
PO BOX 1341
BUFFALO NY 14240-8571

NO POSTAGE
NECESSARY
IF MAILED
IN THE
UNITED STATES

"I know money is tight. Joe has an old retired rodeo buddy who can do the job."

"Don't you think I need a licensed electrician?"

"Connor, that's his name, is fully licensed and insured. After he got injured, he left the rodeo circuit and got licensed so he could work in the family business. Joe said he does great work."

"Still, I'll need to get a couple of estimates. As you said, my budget is tight."

Luke shook his head. "Connor will do the work at no charge."

Meg shook her head. "I couldn't allow that. It wouldn't be fair to expect him to work for free. It's bad enough I'm taking advantage of you and Joe by not paying either of you."

"You're not taking advantage of us. As for Connor, he's like the rest of us on the rodeo circuit. We're one big family. When someone needs help, we join together and do what we can. That's what we do." It's what he loved most about his profession.

"But I'm not part of the rodeo family. You know as well as anyone that I want to stay far away from that life. It's caused too much pain in my past."

Luke understood. The rodeo was the reason she'd grown up with a father who was never around. "You might not be part of the family, so to speak, but you're a friend of mine, and that's all that matters. I'll be honest with you, hiring an electrician can be very expensive. It would be in your best interest and the children's if you accept Connor's help. Maybe once the repairs are done and the rooms are open again, you can offer a weekend stay for him and his wife. Like a second honeymoon."

Meg rubbed her eyes to brush the tears away. "That's

a good idea. Maybe I can do the same for Joe since he's been such a big help."

"I'm sure he and his wife would love that."

"This is going to delay the opening of the rooms. Do you have any idea on a timeline?"

"It will all depend on that other room. Joe and I had initially planned to finish the hawk's nest before starting on the other, but we need to find out what's going on behind the other walls."

"And if there's more damage?"

"We'll deal with it as quickly as possible. Don't get discouraged. It should only put us behind a few days."

Meg nodded. "I guess I should be thankful that the wiring never started a fire."

The last thing Luke wanted to do was cause added stress for Meg, but he'd seen firsthand what could happen with faulty wiring—back in Colorado a good friend had lost his home and his two young children in a house fire. The fire investigator determined the wiring had been damaged by a family of squirrels that had taken up residency in the attic. He and Joe would make sure that the other room, along with the rest of the house, was safe before they would start any repairs. "The good thing is we found the problem, so we'll get it taken care of. There's no need for you to worry."

"Thank you both for your help. I appreciate it. Now—the kids. I guess I shouldn't put it off any longer."

"Why don't I go down to the barn with you?" Luke offered.

"That won't be necessary, but thank you."

"Maybe not, but I'm part of this fictional story, too. I'd like to hear what they say." Luke winked. "Let me make a quick call to Joe. I'll ask him to reach out to Connor about inspecting the entire house."

Ten minutes later Joe had confirmed with Luke that Connor would handle the inspection first thing in the morning.

Outside, the late afternoon sun hung low over the mountains. Meg was quiet as the two strolled down the trampled path to the larger of the two barns.

Luke took in his surroundings. "This property would be perfect for a few animals. Have you ever thought about adding a horse or two? It might be an activity that would draw more guests to the B&B. And the barn—it's huge. It would make a great wedding venue."

"What? Not you, too. Everyone I spoke with today who thought we were getting married said the B&B would be the perfect spot."

"I agree." Luke paused and grinned. "Not about our marriage, but it would be a nice place to host weddings. There's a lot of money to be made in that industry. Don't tell me you've never thought about it."

"Yes, when I first took over the B&B, I did think about it. I imagined offering sleigh rides in the winter, weddings in the spring and horseback excursions during the summer months. But once I realized the financial situation of the property, I had to stop trying to romanticize the B&B as some magical getaway. I wanted to target newlyweds planning their wedding and couples celebrating their anniversary. It all sounds kind of silly."

"Why would you say that? It seems like a good idea to me."

Meg hesitated before answering. "I don't think I'm the best person to be promoting love and relationships, since it's not something I believe in anymore. But I do think it was all part of Gina's vision and what she wanted for the B&B."

Luke's stomach twisted into a knot. Was he the reason Meg no longer believed in love and marriage? Or had somebody come along after him and hurt her even more? "I think you're too young to give up on love."

Meg shrugged her shoulders. "I don't feel comfortable talking about this with you. Besides, making upgrades to the B&B and the property would take a lot of money."

Luke saw a lot of promise in the business. "I could help you." As soon as he said it, he noticed Meg's shoulders straighten.

"You want to give me money? What makes you think I would accept financial assistance from you?"

"Not give it to you, invest. My financial adviser is always telling me to look for good opportunities to invest my money. I don't have a family or a lot of financial obligations."

"You're not serious, are you?"

"Why not? It would be good for you and also for the community. You might not believe me, but Whispering Slopes will always be my home. Its economic well-being is important to me."

Meg remained silent. Maybe she didn't trust him. But if she'd read the letter, she'd have no reason not to. This was strictly a business deal—nothing more. "Will you at least think about it?"

As they neared the barn, they could hear laughter and giggles coming from inside. Within seconds, the joyful sounds were replaced by a scream and then whimpering.

Without hesitation, both Luke and Meg took off running down the path. Once outside the barn, Luke pushed the door open. His adrenaline surged when he spotted Tia on the ground holding her arm and crying. Her face was red and wet with tears.

Meg raced to her and dropped to the ground. "Tell me what hurts, sweetie."

"My arm," the child wailed. "I was on Tucker's back. I couldn't hold on anymore."

Meg threw a glance toward Luke. Her eyes were daggers. The children had been mutton busting. This was all his fault.

"I didn't mean to do it!" Tucker cried out. "Tia told me she wanted me to buck up and down harder, so I did. I'm sorry, Tia."

Luke moved toward the boy and rubbed his shoulder. "I'm sure you didn't mean it."

Tia's cries quieted, but she continued to hold her right arm. "It hurts."

Luke turned to Meg. "We need to get her checked out. I'll get my truck. Leave her there. I'll pick her up and carry her to the car."

Meg nodded.

"Where are you taking me?" Tia whimpered.

"We're going to the emergency room so the doctor can look at your arm. Don't worry, I'll stay with you the entire time." Meg gently bushed her lips against Tia's cheek. "You'll be fine."

Luke bolted from the barn and raced to his truck. He sent up a silent prayer for Tia. If she was seriously injured, he would never forgive himself. Was Meg right? Had it been a mistake to introduce the children to rodeo life?

Chapter Nine

The emergency room at Shenandoah Memorial Hospital felt more like a library than a medical facility. Had it been a Saturday, the area would be filled with patients suffering from sports-related injuries.

"What's going to happen now, Aunt Meg?" The large gurney swallowed Tia's tiny frame as the two waited in the examination room.

Meg inched her chair closer. She extended her hand and brushed her niece's hair away from her face. "We're waiting to see the doctor. He'll examine your arm and probably take a couple of X-rays."

Tia's brow crinkled. "What's that? It sounds scary." She tucked the sheet closer to her chin.

"There's nothing to be afraid of, sweetie. An X-ray is only a picture of your bone."

"But my skin covers my bones. Will they have to cut my arm first?"

"Oh, no, it's nothing like that. The machine can see through the top of your skin to take a picture. I've had several of them. I had my first X-ray when I was your age."

Tia's eyes widened. "Really? Did you hurt your arm, too?"

"No, I was climbing a rope in gym class. When I jumped down, I twisted my ankle."

"Ouch. That must have hurt." Tia rubbed her arm. "It doesn't feel as bad as it did back in the barn. What happened to your ankle?"

"Well, it turned out I had broken my foot. But the doctor put a cast on it, and after six weeks my foot was as good as new."

"Will I have to have a cast?"

Meg hoped there were no broken bones. "We have to wait and see what the X-ray shows. But wearing a cast isn't that big of a deal. They make them different now. When I had mine, it was made out of a material that allowed my friends to write on it."

Tia's brow furrowed. "What kind of stuff did they write?"

Meg smiled as she recalled what Luke had written. *I'm sorry you got hurt.* Then he'd drawn a tiny heart next to his name. "Just silly things. Some of my friends drew funny faces next to their names, while others just wrote they hoped I'd get better soon."

Tia smiled. "Cool. I wish I could have a cast like that."

"Well let's just say a prayer that your arm will be fine. Trust me, the novelty of wearing a cast wears off quickly." Meg recalled how miserable she was when her foot would start to itch in the middle of the night. Her mother had given her a spoon to keep on her nightstand. Meg would slide the utensil between her skin and the cast, but the spoon never quite reached the itch.

"Maybe it would be cool for a week." Tia giggled. She bit down on her lower lip and looked up. "Don't be mad at Tucker for what happened. It wasn't his fault. He and Tilly were having so much fun, I begged him to let me try. I kept telling him to go faster and lift me off the ground higher like he did with Tilly. Tucker thinks I'm not as tough as her—maybe I'm not. But I'm not a chicken."

Meg's anger was directed toward Luke. He'd gone against her wishes about keeping the rodeo out of the children's minds. She couldn't deny that she was thrilled Tucker seemed to be doing better, but now with Tia injured, she was having reservations about allowing Luke to take him to the camp on Saturday.

"I'm not mad at Tucker, sweetie. I know it was an accident."

"We're ready to take you back to X-ray."

Meg turned to the young nurse who had stepped into the room.

Tia squeezed Meg's arm. "I'm scared. Can you go with me?"

Meg made eye contact with the young woman.

"Of course your mommy can go with you." The nurse smiled.

"She's not my mommy. She's my aunt. But can she still go?"

Tia was right. She wasn't the children's mother. At times she felt guilty for wishing they called her mommy instead of aunt.

The nurse raised the bars on the side of the gurney then gripped the handles behind Tia's head. "Yes, your aunt can go with you."

Thirty minutes later, Meg scanned the emergency room for Luke and the children. She spotted Tucker and Tilly working on a jigsaw puzzle in the children's area. Her eyes moved across the room in search of Luke. Her breath caught in her throat when she spotted him staring at her from across the room. For a second, her pulse accelerated like it had when she was a young girl and head over heels for a boy named Luke. She shook off the feeling and worked her way across the room to where he stood. She needed to leave that girl behind where she belonged.

Luke met her halfway. "How's Tia doing?"

"She was a little scared at first, but she's okay now. We're just waiting on the doctor to read the X-ray. The poor little thing. She fell asleep while I was reading her a story, so I thought I'd slip out and give you an update." Meg glanced over toward the kids. "Thanks for keeping an eye on them."

"Sure. No problem. They've been staying busy with the puzzle. Let's go have a seat while we wait." Luke reached for her arm and guided her to the chairs lining the back wall.

Once seated, Meg watched as Tilly whispered something into Tucker's ear. They both looked toward her and Luke and giggled.

"I just hope nothing is broken. She doesn't seem to be in that much pain now, so hopefully, that's a good sign."

Luke dropped his gaze to the floor. "I'm sorry. I know you're not happy that the kids were pretending to be mutton busting when Tia got hurt, but I hope this doesn't change your mind about me taking Tucker to the camp on Saturday."

"The thought crossed my mind. But as much as I don't want to admit it, I do think your time spent with him has helped. If that involves two Saturdays at a mutton camp, I guess I'll just have to grin and bear it."

"I'm glad you feel that way. You won't regret it. I promise."

Across the room, the giggles once again caught Meg's

attention. She had a feeling she knew what the kids were whispering about.

"What's up with them?" Luke glanced at the play area, where the children continued to whisper and giggle.

"I'm not sure, but I hope they're not cooking up more rumors to spread around town. I should go talk to them. I don't think this can wait. I'll speak with Tia when she's feeling better. I need to put an end to this rumor."

"Let's both go." Luke stood and extended his hand to help her from the chair.

More giggles erupted. Meg pulled her hand away. "See—we're giving the kids the wrong impression."

At the table, Meg observed Tucker and Tilly. They both had their heads down and focused on the puzzle.

Tucker looked up first. "Is Tia going to be okay? Will she have to stay here overnight? I can stay with her if she's scared."

Meg slipped into the empty chair next to Tilly and crossed her hand on her lap. "We're waiting to hear from the doctor. They took an X-ray, which is a picture of her arm, to make sure she doesn't have any broken bones. As for staying over tonight, I don't think that's going to be necessary."

Tucker looked up at Meg. The corners of his mouth turned downward. "I didn't mean to hurt her. We were just messing around. I thought she was having fun."

"I know you didn't intentionally do anything wrong. Sometimes accidents happen."

"Am I going to be grounded? I don't want to miss the mutton busting camp on Saturday." Tucker rubbed his eyes.

Meg glanced at Luke, who remained quiet.

"No, you're not grounded. I know that you're looking forward to your day with Mr. Luke. I want you to go and have fun."

Tucker's face brightened. "Thank you. I can't wait!" His smile dulled. "You're not coming, too, are you?"

Meg tried not to let Tucker's question hurt her feelings, but it did. "No, I won't be going. You know I'm not a big fan of the rodeo. Why would you think I would go?"

Tucker tossed a glance at his sister. Tilly's eyes widened.

"Do you want to tell me what's going on?" Meg's eyes zeroed in on Tilly.

"Nothing." The little girl shrugged her shoulders.

Hold your peace. One of them will cave.

Tucker squirmed in the chair. "We just thought you would go, too—since you and Cowboy Luke are dating."

"Tuck!" Tilly reached across the table for his hand.

"What would make you think Mr. Luke and I are dating?" Meg directed her question to Tucker with hopes that she'd get more information from him.

"Well…ah…we saw you holding hands." Tucker kept his head down.

"And? Is there any other reason?"

"You guys are together a lot. Like all the time," Tucker added.

Meg waited for him to continue building his defense.

"Tilly and Tia told me!" The boy crossed his arms over his chest.

Now she was getting somewhere.

Luke slipped into the last empty chair on the other side of Tucker.

Meg cleared her throat and addressed Tilly. "Why would you make up a story like that and then tell your brother?"

"Tia did it, too," Tilly answered.

"Well, she's not here to defend herself, so right now I'm asking you the question."

Tilly kept her lower lip rolled down and firm.

Meg leaned in closer. "You don't have an answer for me?"

The child shrugged her shoulders. "I guess the same reasons Tuck said."

"So, is this why you told your classmates that Mr. Luke and I are getting married?"

Tilly's eyes popped. "You know?"

Luke chuckled.

Meg wasn't sure what Luke found so funny. This was far from amusing.

"Yes, I do. And today I discovered practically the whole town knows, too."

Tilly's lips moved into the shape of the letter O. "But I only told a couple of kids in school."

"I've told some, too," Tucker confessed.

"Well, they told some more kids and those kids probably told their parents and so on. You know we live in a small town. You have to be careful what you say to other people. You don't want to have the reputation of being someone who spreads gossip."

Tucker bit his lower lip. "How can I spread something when I don't even know what it means?"

"Gossip is when someone tells you something and you don't know for sure if it's true. But even though you aren't sure, you tell someone else anyway. If you listen to someone telling you gossip, believe me, that same person will gossip about you, too. Gossip can be very hurtful to a person."

Meg remembered her freshman year in high school. For a week her mother refused to get out of bed after someone in town told her that her husband had been seeing another woman while on tour with the rodeo. Meg had never believed her father would do that to her mother—to his family. In the end, her mother ended up leaving her father. She claimed rodeo life created emotional distress. Once the divorce was final, her mom immediately remarried a man she had been secretly seeing before she left her father. Maybe if her father hadn't been on the road with the rodeo so often, her mother wouldn't have felt the need to find another man.

Silence circled the table.

Tucker picked up a piece of the puzzle and examined it before he looked up at Meg. "I didn't mean to hurt you." Then he turned to Luke. "Or you, either. I just—"

"What is it?" Meg gently placed her hand on the child's back.

Tucker placed the piece back on the table and gazed out the window overlooking the courtyard. "I just want to have a family again. So we can fix the tree." Tucker rubbed his hand up his arm.

Meg looked at Luke. He shrugged his shoulders. "What tree are you talking about, sweetie?" Meg asked.

"Our family tree. Like the one we made in school right before everything changed. With Mommy and Daddy gone, the branch is broken. The tree will end up dying." Tucker wiped a tear from his cheek.

His words pierced Meg's heart. She remembered that feeling as a little girl, longing for her father to return from the tour. The sounds of passing cars constantly drew her to the window.

"Why can't you and Cowboy Luke get married? Then you can fix the tree," he blurted in a loud tone.

Meg's cheeks burned when Luke turned his focus to her.

"Well, first of all, Mr. Luke doesn't live here. He's only visiting for now."

"But we could move." Tilly shook her head. "I can make new friends in Colorado."

"Yeah, and I can become a rodeo star like Cowboy Luke." Tucker jumped on the bandwagon.

This was getting way out of control. "Of course, we could all move—"

"Yay! I'm going to start packing as soon as we get home. I can pack Tia's stuff if her arm still hurts too bad."

Luke covered his mouth to conceal his smile. There was no hiding it from Meg. She could tell by the way his eyes crinkled. She'd always loved his eyes.

Meg cleared her throat and attempted to take control of the conversation. "You didn't let me finish. Yes, we could all move to Colorado, but getting married involves more than logistics. You have to love the other person."

"But Lisa's mommy said you used to love Cowboy Luke. She even said you were supposed to get married. If you loved him before, why can't you love him now?"

"Miss Brennan." The nurse who had taken Tia back to X-ray stepped into the waiting room. "The doctor is ready to speak with you now."

Meg was relieved to escape Tilly's question. She couldn't have gotten out of the waiting room any faster if there had been a fire. As she followed the nurse down the hallway, the walls seemed to be closing in on her. Tilly had been right. She had loved Luke. More than anything or anyone she'd ever loved before or since. This was exactly why she needed Luke to return to Colorado as soon as he was healed. She couldn't allow him to take space in her heart once again.

* * *

"Connor is almost finished with the wiring, so we should be able to get the drywall up before the end of the day." Joe strolled into the hawk's nest carrying a thermos and two paper cups.

Gallons of caffeine was exactly what he needed following a restless night of sleep. Luke inhaled the aroma. Since he'd returned from his physical therapy appointment with Meg earlier this morning, he'd been hard at work tearing down the drywall in the hawk's nest. The improvement in his neck served as a reminder that his time in Whispering Slopes would soon come to an end. Meg was helping him recover, but could he help her heal the wounds she carried from their past? He'd opened his heart to her in the letter, but that hadn't changed her feelings. At this point, what more could he do?

The scene at the hospital yesterday had been uncomfortable for Meg. After she'd spoken with the doctor and found out Tia only had a slight sprain, the topic of the girls gossiping wasn't brought up during the car ride home. Meg never spoke a word to him.

"Have you told Meg the good news about the wiring?" Joe placed the cups on the table and filled each to the brim.

"No, she's still in town. She had a jammed scheduled today."

Luke had been relieved when Connor determined that, unlike the hawk's nest, the eagle's nest and the rest of the house had no damage to the wiring. If it was a critter that had done the damage in the other room, maybe it had gotten its fill. Thankfully, it was one less thing for Meg to worry about. She had a lot on her plate.

Those thoughts had been part of the reason he had

spent a restless night tossing and turning. Not only was
he worried about Meg's financial situation and how
Tucker would behave once Luke returned to Colorado,
but he had concerns about her living on the property
alone with the children. Sure, guests were coming and
going, but what about those nights when the B&B was
vacant? He'd had an idea in the wee hours of the morning, but he had to run it by Meg first. He turned to Joe.
"Earlier, I heard Connor mention some German shepherd puppies."

"Yeah, and boy, are they adorable, but there's only
two left. His shepherd Lilly had a litter about eight
weeks ago. Do you think you might be interested?"

Luke had come close to buying a dog last year, but
being on the rodeo circuit wasn't conducive to having pets. True, he was blessed that as adults he and his
brothers built a close bond with each other. They all had
separate houses on a three-thousand-acre farm they'd
inherited from their mother's sister, but he couldn't ask
his brothers to take care of his pets every time he had
to leave town for a competition. Even though his oldest
brother, Jake, a dog lover and breeder, had told Luke
he'd be more than happy to take care of a dog when
Luke was out of town.

"No, not for me. I thought once I'm gone, it might be
a good idea for Tucker to have a dog as his companion.
Plus it could provide security for Meg and the kids."

Joe took a sip of his coffee and smiled. "You could always stay in Whispering Slopes and protect them yourself." He winked.

"I'm not sure Meg would go for that idea."

"But what about you? You're not going to stand there
and tell me that you don't still have feelings for her, are
you? I've seen you two together."

Joe's comment triggered a jolt of joy. He couldn't deny that those thoughts had crept into his mind since he'd returned to his hometown. But as quickly as they'd slipped in, Luke had to force them away. If Meg hadn't forgiven him by now, she never would. "That was a long time ago, buddy. Some things aren't meant to be."

"I don't know, man. The two of you seem to be getting along okay to me. She's allowing you to live under the same roof."

"Meg has a good head for business. She knew it would help her financially if I stayed as a guest at the B&B. But after Tia took a fall, I can tell she's having second thoughts about me taking Tucker to the mutton busting camp tomorrow. She's afraid the boy will want to grow up to be a cowboy."

Joe laughed. "Give her time. She'll see cowboys aren't so bad. You couldn't ask for a more close-knit family than the rodeo community."

"I don't think she ever opened her eyes to that when she was younger. Meg was just a little girl who wanted her father home and not always on tour. Bringing a dog into the house could get Tucker's focus off the rodeo. Maybe I'll talk to Connor about his pups."

"Remember, he only has two left from the litter, so you better talk to him sooner rather than later."

Out front, a car door slammed. Luke glanced through the window and spotted Meg exiting the vehicle. "It looks like it could be sooner. She's home."

"Go ahead and talk to her. I've got everything under control in here. Maybe you should tell her about the wiring first. It might put her in a more receptive mood to the puppy idea."

"My thoughts exactly." Luke laughed. He took another swig of his coffee, placed the cup on the table, and headed outside.

From the porch he noticed Meg juggling a few bags along with her briefcase. He descended the steps and jogged toward her. "Here, let me help you."

"Thanks. I had to run by the market to pick up a couple of things for dinner tonight."

Luke stuck his face inside one of the bags. "Anything good?" he joked in an attempt to lighten the mood.

Meg laughed. "If you like cauliflower, carrots and broccoli—then yes."

Luke crinkled his nose. "I was kind of hoping for something with sugar. I've still got that sweet tooth."

"You grabbed the wrong bag." She swung the one she was holding up toward him. "This one's got a chocolate cake."

"With white icing? That's always been my favorite." On his sixteenth birthday, Meg had shown up at his front door early in the morning. She'd had a cluster of colorful balloons in one hand and a cake in the other.

"Of course the icing is white."

Had she remembered that was his favorite? Or was it just a coincidence?

"It's Tia's favorite."

His heart sank. He should've known better. After he'd walked out on her, she'd probably erased everything she ever knew about him. Or maybe she'd never really cared in the first place.

Meg locked the vehicle. "I felt sorry for her when she left for school today wearing the sling on her little arm."

"Well, if it makes you feel any better when she got home, she raced upstairs to tell me and Joe how cool all her friends thought she looked wearing it."

Meg's face brightened, and she laughed. "Aren't children funny?"

Luke nodded. "I remember when you broke your foot and everyone was signing your cast. I was a little jealous of all the attention you were getting. I wondered if I could buy a fake cast and pretend I had a broken bone."

"You certainly don't have to break anything now to get a lot of attention. Look how famous you are. I'm sure you have women throwing themselves at you."

Luke couldn't ignore the sadness in her eyes. "Maybe so, but they're not my type of women."

Silence clung in the air. He wanted to say more, but the truth kept him quiet. When he decided to stay at Meg's B&B, he'd made a promise to himself that he would keep his head closed to any possibility of a reunion.

That option was off the table. Meg's silence had been proof. She didn't realize how painful it had been for him to sit down and reveal the truth of how his parents felt about their youngest son. The writing was on the wall—she didn't care. And perhaps she never had.

Chapter Ten

Meg finished putting the groceries away and went to work on the salad she planned to serve along with the spaghetti for dinner. She appreciated Luke helping her bring in the groceries, but he continued to linger in the kitchen, making her feel uneasy. Was he hoping for a slice of cake? "If you're hanging around thinking that you're going to get your dessert before dinner, you're wasting your time." Meg turned on the faucet and held the head of broccoli under the running water.

She turned as Luke moved toward the drawer that held the utensils and removed a knife. He was learning his way around her kitchen. That couldn't be a good thing.

"I thought I could help you with dinner."

"I appreciate the offer, but I've been doing this on my own since long before you ever arrived." Where did that come from? "I'm sorry. That was rude." Meg took a paper towel from the holder and blotted the vegetable dry before placing it on the cutting board. She picked up the cauliflower and began to rinse it.

"Things move faster when you work together." Luke used the knife to cut off the stem of the broccoli. "Plus, I wanted to talk to you about something."

Meg's shoulders stiffened. She hoped he wasn't going to bring up the discussion that had happened at the emergency room. That was something she'd rather forget.

"Don't worry, I'm not going to ask you out on a date or anything." Luke laughed.

There had been a time when Meg dreamed of Luke asking her to go out with him. They had grown up together as playmates. The best of friends. That changed when Luke had surprised Meg with an invitation to attend their junior prom as his date. He'd made a point of saying they'd go as boyfriend and girlfriend. Not just friends.

By that time, Meg already harbored a secret crush on Luke, but she believed he'd only thought of her as his best bud. Everything changed after their first kiss. Meg wrote every night in her journal about how she couldn't wait to marry Luke and raise a family. She thought he had wanted it, too. In the end, he wanted to be a rodeo star more.

"Don't even joke about that. I had a long talk with the girls last night when I put them into bed. I made it clear that once you have recovered, you will be heading back to Colorado."

"That's part of what I wanted to talk to you about."

Meg's stomach twisted. She hoped he hadn't changed his mind about returning home. But why would he? Shortly after Luke left to chase his dream, his mother's sister passed away, leaving Luke and his brothers a large chunk of land in Colorado. It wasn't long after that his parents and three brothers all moved out west. There was nothing here for him in Whispering Slopes. Meg busied her hands opening the bag of carrots and pouring them into the colander. "What's up?"

"Actually, there are two things. But don't worry, the first is great news."

"I could use a little of that."

"Connor checked all the wiring in the house this morning. It appears your visitor must have gotten his fill in the hawk's nest and left. He didn't find any evidence of damaged wire anywhere else in the house, so Joe and I moved forward with replacing the drywall in the eagle's nest."

Meg's shoulders relaxed. "It's great to have some good news for a change. I'd like to do something to show my appreciation for Connor. It was nice of him to help me out—for all of you. I could have never afforded all the repairs on my own."

"We're glad to do it." Luke resumed cutting the vegetables. "That's kind of the other thing I wanted to talk to you about. Being on your own."

Being on her own was something she was used to. It had been that way since she'd gone off to college. She had friends and even dated now and then, but she never allowed any of those relationships to go any further. Although her heart had been open once, she hadn't found the strength to do it again. She planned to enjoy the years with the children until they grew up, went away to college, and had families of their own. Thinking that far in advance often triggered waves of sadness, so she focused on living in the moment and not on a future alone. "When I lived in Richmond, I had financial security. I was always able to provide for myself. Adding three children into the equation has been a juggling act."

"I'm sure it's been a life-changing experience, but I wasn't referring to your financial security. I was thinking about being on your own again dealing with Tucker. I'm sure you've noticed we've become buddies."

Meg wasn't exactly thrilled by this turn of events. Sure, she was happy to see Tucker enjoying himself, but why did it have to be with Luke? "I realize that."

"I thought it might be a good idea to get Tucker a dog. It could provide him with companionship and help him continue to get past the pain of his parents leaving."

Meg had considered the idea when she first took over the B&B. Growing up, her family always had a dog. "The first couple weeks I was here, I thought about getting a dog. Poor Tucker was so distraught. I thought maybe that would help him."

"I think it's worth a try. Connor mentioned his German shepherd had a litter eight weeks ago. He's found homes for all of them except for two. Caring for a puppy and watching it grow might help Tucker adjust to his parents being gone. Plus, once the dog is trained, a shepherd could protect you and the kids when you're here alone."

Meg smiled remembering her German shepherd, Finn. Her father had brought him home as a puppy for added security. At first her mother had objected, but then she liked the fact that Finn guarded the house when her husband was on tour.

"This might be a good idea." Meg noticed the surprised expression on Luke's face. "You were expecting me to say no, weren't you?"

Luke cut the last of the cauliflower. "I was. I know you have a lot going on, and a puppy can be a lot of work. I can help you while I'm here. Hopefully, by the time I leave, the children will take over some of the responsibility."

A rush of excitement filled Meg. "When can we go see the puppies?"

"I thought we could go tomorrow after Tucker and

I get back from camp. I'll give Connor a call to see if that works for him."

Luke's concern for Tucker's well-being warmed Meg's heart, but her excitement for the outing quickly dulled. She couldn't help but wonder why he hadn't been as concerned about her happiness when he up and left town. Did he ever really love her?

"'Hop on and hang on.' That's what Mr. Baker said to do, and I did it! It was only for seven seconds, but I did it. I could go longer if I keep practicing." Tucker skipped alongside Luke as the two headed across the grounds at the Baker Busting Camp.

Luke had woken up early Saturday morning, excited for the day. And so far, it had exceeded his expectations. Tucker had been a bundle of energy, chatting nonstop since climbing into Luke's truck and heading to the camp. Upon their arrival, Tucker mingled with the other children as though they were his best friends.

The day had also stirred up Luke's dream of one day opening a rodeo camp for children. No doubt, he and Tucker weren't the only ones who'd felt abandoned by their parents. Sadly, Luke knew there were probably countless kids who suffered in silence. Children struggling in that type of environment could only benefit from a camp such as this. Tucker's breakthrough was proof enough. Not to mention his own after his uncle took the time to introduce him to the rodeo.

The camp had also sparked another idea—a way to help Meg raise some fast cash. It would take some convincing, but Luke was confident his plan could get the B&B out of debt and making a profit.

Luke rested his hand on Tucker's shoulder. "You did great, son. I'm proud of you."

Tucker stopped in his tracks and looked up at Luke. "I wish you could be my new daddy."

Luke's throat tightened. Had he known Tucker would have had this kind of reaction to his choice of words, he would have chosen them more wisely. "I should have said buddy. I know you're not my son, but sometimes older adults use it as a term of endearment."

He was rambling. Tucker probably didn't know what a term of endearment meant. Meg had warned him about Tucker getting attached, but she hadn't cautioned him about his feelings.

Tucker shrugged his shoulders. "I know I have a daddy, but he doesn't want to be around me, so maybe it's time for me to find a replacement."

Since Tucker had lassoed Luke's heart, he couldn't think of anything better than being Tucker's father. Raising the boy as his own and proving to Tucker that he was loved would be a responsibility Luke wouldn't take for granted. In other words, doing exactly the opposite of what his parents did for him.

No. He wouldn't allow the actions of his parents to ruin their day. He reached for Tucker's hand and headed toward the grill for a couple of sirloin burgers. "Let's go eat." Luke gazed down at Tucker. Surprise took hold as he found himself longing to call Tucker his son.

Chapter Eleven

Late Saturday afternoon, Luke navigated his truck along the zigzagging mountain road to Connor Nolan's farm. Meg listened to the excited chatter coming from the back seat. The afternoon was glorious with bright sunshine and a light breeze. The perfect day to welcome the new puppy into their home. At least that's what Meg kept telling herself. Since she'd agreed to Luke's suggestion, she'd wondered if she was taking on too much. Training a puppy while at the same time raising three children and trying to keep both businesses afloat suddenly felt overwhelming.

"You should have seen me, Aunt Meg." Tucker leaned forward from the back seat. "I fell off after one second on my first ride. But then the trainer showed us kids a few tricks, and by the third run I hung on to the sheep for seven seconds! It was amazing! Mr. Luke said I did the best of all the kids in the camp."

Luke threw a glance in Meg's direction. He'd been right about mutton busting bringing Tucker back to life. She could only hope that a new puppy would be a distraction that would keep his mind off the rodeo.

Tilly leaned forward from her car seat situated between her brother and sister. "When can me and Tia go to camp?"

Tia remained quiet. She'd rather watch than be a participant.

"I don't think you'll be able to go, Til. When the camp comes back next spring, Cowboy Luke will be gone." Tucker's tone sounded less joyful.

Meg glanced in the back and noticed the sadness that had taken over Tilly's face. She didn't respond to Tucker's words, instead turning her gaze toward the window. This was exactly what Meg didn't want to happen—the children getting attached to Luke and being left heart-broken when he went back to Colorado.

The excitement in the cab of the truck quieted, but only for a second. Tucker was too keyed up from the camp experience. "Can't you tell us where we're going?"

"Your aunt Meg wants it to be a surprise," Luke responded over his shoulder. "Don't you like surprises?"

"Not all surprises are good ones," Tucker answered.

"Well, you can trust me. You guys are going to love this one."

Luke's words ignited the level of excitement once again. Meg settled against the leather seat. There was no turning back now. Like it or not, they would be welcoming a puppy into the family.

Twenty minutes later, Luke's truck moved along the winding dirt driveway lined with colorful wildflowers.

"Look at all the cows over there!" Tilly shouted. "There's hundreds of them. I hope there's some horses, too."

Tucker pressed his face to the window. "Do you think there'll be some sheep? If there are, maybe I can show you how good I am at mutton busting."

Meg glanced at Luke, who kept his eyes on the road and slowly navigated the truck in front of the two-story farmhouse with a large wraparound porch lined with white rocking chairs.

Luke brought the vehicle to a stop and turned off the engine. "Okay, kids—let's go and check out the surprise." Luke turned to Meg. "Connor said he'd meet us down at the barn."

They approached the barn following a short walk through the grassy meadow. Connor exited his barn and threw up a wave. On his heels were two rambunctious puppies with large paws and heads that overpowered their small bodies.

"Puppies—cool!" Tucker called out. The children took off running toward the animals.

"Hey, Connor. Thanks for letting us come out this afternoon." The two men shook hands.

"Hi, Meg." Connor smiled.

"Hello. They're adorable." Meg leaned against the wooden railing.

"Is this the surprise?" Tucker called out.

The adults moved closer to the children.

Meg nodded. "Yes, I thought it was about time we add a dog to our family."

The children erupted in cheers.

"Do we really get to take one home?" Tilly giggled as one of the puppies squirmed in her arms and smothered her face with sloppy kisses.

"How do we decide which one to take?" Tucker had the other puppy on his lap. The dogs wiggled to get free. "I think we should take both!"

Meg shook her head. "We're here for one."

Connor slipped his hands in the pockets of his jeans. "I guess you can decide if you want a boy or a girl."

"We want the girl!" Tilly and Tia shouted at once.

Meg watched Tucker scratching the head of the male puppy.

"We already have enough girls in the house. I vote for a boy." Tucker looked up at Luke. "Don't you agree? After you're gone, it will be just me again."

Luke glanced in Meg's direction. "He has a good point."

Meg agreed. "Girls? Do you agree with Tucker?"

Connor knelt beside the children. "If it makes it any easier, I know the Capello family is interested in the female."

"We play with Jordan and Tyler at their house sometimes. We could visit the girl dog," Tilly suggested to her sister.

Tia nodded.

"That sounds like a great idea." Meg looked at Connor. "We officially have a new addition to the family. We'll take the male."

They all said their goodbyes to Connor, who had offered a large cage to transport the puppy to his new home. With everyone loaded in the vehicle, Meg sent up a silent prayer that the dog would help Tucker adjust to a new life without his parents—and without Luke.

Five minutes into the ride, Meg took in her surroundings and leaned her back against the leather seat. As the truck filled with three happy children, two adults and one excited puppy eased onto the main road and headed toward home, Meg's heart squeezed. It felt as though they were a family. She tried to push away the thought, but it gripped her mind for the entire drive home.

Luke woke early Thursday morning stiff and groggy. The past three days, he and Joe had worked from sunup to sundown trying to get the rooms ready so Meg could reopen two weeks from Saturday. In addition, he'd also had a therapy session on Monday and another yesterday. Meg had done some new manipulations on his neck.

Boy, was he feeling it this morning. He swung his feet over the edge of the bed and rubbed his neck. Nothing that a good hot shower wouldn't cure.

A whimper sounded outside his bedroom door, followed by scratching. Luke's bare feet padded across the hardwood floor. The second he opened the door, a brown furry blur zipped over his feet and across the room. With his nose down, the puppy worked to cover every square inch of the floor.

Luke squatted. "Come here, Rocky." The animal froze, spun around and ran full speed into Luke's arms. On Saturday, during the drive home from Connor's farm, everyone agreed to allow Tucker to name the family dog. Without hesitation, he'd come up with Rocky. It was perfect.

"Rocky!" Bare feet slapped against the floor.

Luke peered down the hall and spotted Tucker searching for the dog.

Tucker arrived outside Luke's door breathless. "There you are. I've been looking all over for you."

Luke handed the puppy to Tucker. "I think he came in here to look for some breakfast."

"Sorry. Aunt Meg said I have to take him outside for a walk before I feed him." Tucker buried his face into the dog's coat then looked up at Luke. "Do you want to go with me before the school bus comes?"

There was no way he could say no. "Give me a couple of minutes to jump in the shower. I'll be right with you, buddy."

Tucker's face brightened, and he gave several quick nods.

Following a quick shower, Luke slipped on his cowboy boots and headed outside to meet Tucker.

Minutes later, Luke pulled in a lungful of the crisp

mountain air. He and Tucker moved down the path at a brisk pace to keep up with Rocky.

"Do you think it would be okay if I let him off the leash?" Tucker stumbled on a root, temporarily losing his stride.

Luke had a feeling if Rocky had a chance to run free, he might keep going until he crossed the state line. "I think it's best to keep him on the leash until he's out of the rambunctious puppy stage."

"When do you think that will be?" Tucker squinted up into the bright sunshine.

Bringing a puppy into the home had been his idea, so it was only fair that he'd help train the dog. Meg didn't have time with her busy schedule. Hopefully, once the two rooms were reopened, she'd keep them booked with the guests. Meg needed a steady stream of income to help ease some of her financial worries. He admired her loyalty to her sister. Maintaining the promise to keep the B&B open for the children was important to Meg.

"I thought you and I could start training Rocky after school today."

Tucker's sleepy eyes popped. "Really? You want to help me?"

Luke ran his hand over the top of Tucker's head. "Sure. I've raised a few pups in my lifetime. You want to start the training as soon as possible before they develop too many bad habits."

"Maybe we can teach him how to fetch a ball first."

Luke shook his head. "There's something more important that all dogs should learn first."

Tucker's brow creased. "What's that?"

"If you want to let Rocky run free, you have to teach him how to come before you remove the leash."

"How do we do that?" Rocky's pace increased, pulling Tucker's arm. "Hold on. Not so fast."

"We'll practice by asking him to come and then repeating his name," Luke explained.

"That sounds pretty easy. That's it?"

"Not exactly. Rocky will need to be rewarded when he does something good."

"What kind of a reward? Like a pat on the head?"

"Most puppies will respond best to treats." Luke brushed the top of Tucker's head. "Kind of like kids. I'll run by the store and pick up some doggy snacks that we can use. Maybe liver."

Tucker crinkled up his nose. "Yuck. I sure wouldn't come for that. I don't know if Rocky would like it, either."

Luke laughed. "You might be surprised. Most dogs love liver."

"Blah. I'm glad I'm not a dog. So, what do we do after Rocky comes to us and we feed him a treat?"

"We'll keep expanding the distance, so I'll need to pick up a longer leash, too. We can't take any chance of him running off."

Tucker sighed. "I wish I could've kept my parents on a leash."

Luke's heart broke for the young boy.

"Do you think they'll ever come back? Maybe Aunt Meg can write them a letter and tell them how good I'm doing in school. I haven't been in a fight in over a week." He paused for a moment and bit down on his lower lip. "And last week I didn't miss one word on my spelling test."

"Let's go have a seat over there. I think Rocky's legs could use a break." Luke pointed to the grassy slope that looked down over the pond.

Tucker flopped down on the ground while Luke secured the leash to a nearby tree trunk. Rocky barked and flopped down on the grass.

Tucker pulled his knees up to his chest and exhaled. "This is where my daddy and I used to come to fish. He'd tell me stories about fishing with his daddy."

Luke took in the scenery. "It's a great spot. Maybe you and I can come back here and do some fishing together."

"What's the point?"

"What do you mean?"

Tucker remained silent with his fists underneath his chin.

"Come on. Talk to me. We're supposed to be buddies, remember? Why wouldn't you want to go fishing with me?"

"You're just going to leave, too—like my parents."

Oh boy. Meg had warned him about this. "That's true. Eventually, I need to return to Colorado, but that doesn't mean I won't come back to visit. And we can talk on the phone, too."

"You say that now, but once you're gone, you'll forget about me. I'm sure my parents have forgotten all about me by now. I guess that's what happens when you're meek. People just forget you."

Luke swallowed hard to force down the lump blocking his throat. "I doubt your parents have forgotten you."

"I don't," Tucker was quick to respond. "They haven't even called once. I just want to talk to my daddy and tell him if they come home, I'll keep being good. I'll keep my room clean. I'll even brush my teeth three times a day. I just want to have a family again."

Luke needed to make Tucker realize his parents' choice to leave had nothing to do with him. But how?

He'd struggled with the same thoughts. "Your parents didn't leave because of anything that you did or didn't do."

"How do you know?"

He didn't. How could he give Tucker advice when he still questioned what he could've done to get his parents to love him for who he was and not because he won competitions? "I felt the same way you did when I was a kid. I was always trying to do things to please my parents, thinking that my actions could make them love me more."

"Did it work?"

Luke shook his head. Even becoming a famous bull rider wasn't enough to gain unconditional love from his parents. "I was blessed to have an uncle who took the time to teach me about God's unconditional love for His children."

Tucker sat quietly absorbing Luke's words. "Maybe before you leave to go home you can teach me, too."

Luke didn't have the heart to tell Tucker his time in Whispering Slopes would be coming to an end before he'd have a chance to do all the things he'd like to do. Things that could help Meg and her family.

His cell phone rang and pulled him from his thoughts. He glanced at the screen. Reed. His agent. He probably wanted to check in to see how his recovery was going. "Hey, buddy, I need to get this. Keep an eye on Rocky. I'll be right back."

Tucker nodded. "Okay."

Luke stood from the grassy bank. He swiped his phone to accept the call. "Hey, Reed. What's up?"

"I wanted to touch base with you to see how your neck is doing."

Luke had been so busy with the repairs on the rooms

and spending time with the kids, it had been easy to forget about his injury. "I'm still doing physical therapy, but it's improving."

"So, the therapist I hooked you up with is good?"

Reed had no idea Luke and Meg were once high school sweethearts. It was best to keep that information to himself, especially since Reed was always trying to set him up with different women. "Yes, she's been great."

"Excellent. I'm glad to hear that because I have some big news for you."

"Oh yeah?" Luke kept a close eye on Tucker. He was anxious to end the call.

"Well, don't sound too excited there, buddy." Reed laughed. "This could be huge for your career."

"Sorry, man. I just have a lot of things on my mind." That was an understatement. Lately, the idea of leaving Meg and the kids was weighing more heavily on his mind than he'd like. He only hoped that once he went back to Colorado, all the feelings and regrets that had surfaced from his past would subside. "So, what's the news?"

"I've got a big opportunity for you. But you'll need to return to work earlier than you had planned."

Luke's pulse told him he wasn't ready to leave. "How much earlier? I'm still under the physical therapist's care. I don't think she believes I'm ready to ride this soon."

"That's part of the good news. I know you're anxious to compete in the Castle Rock tour, but the opportunity I'm talking about wouldn't involve you getting back on a bull before you're ready. It's a series of truck commercials. And the great thing is, it's the same company that built the truck you drive."

Luke had his fair share of endorsements from big companies, but he had never done commercials. He had a few rodeo buddies who'd made a lot of money going in front of the camera and endorsing products. "I'm not sure that's my style. You know me—once I'm out of the arena, I prefer to keep a low profile." Being in the spotlight wasn't part of Luke's comfort zone.

"Well, you're going to have to get over your stage fright, because what they're offering is big—really big. You might even be able to retire sooner than you talked about."

Retirement had been on his mind lately, especially since the injury to his neck. He wasn't getting any younger. But who would he be if he wasn't a famous bull rider? It was where he found his stability. "What's the earliest I would need to return to Colorado?"

"Actually, you would need to go to Montana first."

"Is that where they want to film the commercial?" Luke had spent some time in Montana, and he even had a few rodeo buddies who had relocated there after retiring.

"It's not just one commercial. It would be a sixteen-month advertising campaign. The company plans to do advertisements at different locations all over the country. Whenever people see one of these trucks on the road, they'll think of you."

Luke had grown more comfortable staying in one place since he'd been back in Whispering Slopes. The thought of a hectic travel schedule wasn't appealing at all. "I'm not sure about this. Can I think about it for a while?"

Silence filled the phone line. Reed wasn't happy.

"What could you possibly have to think about? This

is a huge opportunity for you." He blew out a powerful breath. "You'd be a fool to pass it up."

Reed would also make a nice paycheck if Luke decided to sign on the dotted line. He couldn't blame his agent for trying to put a little pressure on him. "Maybe so, but I still need time to think about it. It sounds like a big commitment."

"Fine. I'll try to buy a little bit more time with the company, but trust me, they've got another cowboy next in line who is chomping at the bit for this deal."

Luke had no doubt that was true. Everyone in this industry was expendable, including himself. "I'll be in touch." Luke wanted to get off the phone as fast as he could and get back with Tucker.

"My advice—don't wait too long."

Luke pressed End on his device, but his agent's offer hung over him like a black cloud. Most people would be thrilled by an offer like this. Why wasn't he happy? He pocketed his phone and glanced at Tucker rolling in the grass. He giggled as Rocky smothered his face with wet kisses. Luke smiled and went toward the child. This was what made him happy. The opportunity that waited for him in Montana couldn't compare.

Chapter Twelve

"I can't believe how much you and Joe have gotten done in only a few days." Meg stood inside the hawk's nest with her hands on her hips, admiring the freshly painted cream-colored walls. "I was in here the other day, and there were giant holes in the walls, and the floors were a mess. Look at it now. I've never seen the hardwood look so luminous." A lump formed in her throat.

"Joe's a good worker. After I mentioned to him that I wanted to get the place ready for your grand reopening two weeks from today, there was no stopping him. I don't think he took one break yesterday."

"I hadn't planned on having a grand reopening." Getting paying guests back to the B&B was her number one priority.

Luke jammed his hands into the front pockets of his worn jeans. "I didn't think so, but it could be a great opportunity to bring in more business and help you pay off the debt your sister left behind. We could host an open house and allow people to come inside and tour the entire B&B. Let them know all that the Trout Run Bed and Breakfast has to offer for a weekend or midweek getaway. We can serve food and drinks and even have games for the kids. Joe said he could write up an announcement for his church newsletter. That way you could draw people from outside Whispering Slopes."

Meg's head whirled as she tried to take in all the information Luke was throwing at her. Of course, paying off the mountain of debt would be a dream come true for her. But right now, it seemed like an impossibility. "You keep saying 'we,' but I haven't agreed to any of this. Besides, there's not enough time to plan everything you're suggesting. It's impossible. Remember, I still have patients to treat, including you."

"Try not to think of it as an event. Just picture it as having some friends over to fellowship."

Meg released a slow breath. "You can think of it any way you'd like, but organizing something like this not only takes time, it costs money. You know I can't afford any extras." Adding another mouth to feed when they adopted Rocky was enough of a strain, but the kids loved the dog. Meg had grown quite attached to the puppy herself. However, it did rattle her nerves to think how much food Rocky would consume as he grew.

"It's not going to cost you anything. Now promise me you won't get mad." Luke hunched his shoulders.

"I'm not so sure I can do that."

"Okay, but I've already spoken with Miss Mattie and Mrs. Buser about the event. They're already planning the menu with their women's group from church."

Heat filled Meg's face. "I can't impose on these women. They have lives and families of their own to care for. They don't have time to cook for me."

"Come on, Meg. You know those ladies live for this stuff. Remember when we were kids and the Jenkinses' house caught fire? Not only did the women in this town give the family a roof over their head and hot meals, but everyone came together and rebuilt their home. This town hasn't changed a bit from when we were kids. When your neighbor has a need, you respond—no questions asked. That's all they're doing for you. It's not charity. One day they might need assistance, and you'd do the same thing."

She couldn't argue with that. The people in this town were like one big family. They were the most loving and caring folks she'd ever known. It's what she'd missed most when she'd moved to Richmond. "But what about all this new paint?" She pointed at the walls. "I have to pay someone for this. Did you buy it or did Joe? I need to write someone a check." But first, she would need to check her bank balance.

"Neither. Joe has a buddy who recently purchased a fixer-upper home. He completely remodeled the entire house. After he purchased all the paint, his wife changed her mind about the color. She wanted a light yellow instead. Joe's friend couldn't get a refund, so he wanted to give it to someone who could use it. Joe tried to give him some money, but he refused to accept any payment."

Meg was touched by the generosity of Luke and his friends. Her father had always told her the cowboy community stuck together and was always there to help those in need. She was seeing that firsthand. Were they any different than the residents in Whispering Slopes? Always willing to lend a hand, expecting nothing in return. "So, is there anything left for me to do?" Meg smiled.

"Not really, but I'll find something for you." Luke nudged his elbow into her arm.

Having someone to work with toward a common

goal was nice. Most of her adult years had been spent handling things on her own. Meg had accepted the fact that this was the way it would be. Trusting her heart to a man wasn't worth the risk. Of course, there was no denying that having Luke around the last couple of weeks had been nice. But no matter how good it felt, she couldn't allow these thoughts to cloud her mind. She and Luke had their chance, but that was all in the past. She refused to allow herself to be that vulnerable again. "Well, thank you again for all your hard work. The place looks great."

Luke scanned the room and nodded. "It will look even better when the rooms are filled with paying guests."

"You're right about that." Meg forced a laugh, unable to get the mountain of bills that continued to pile up while the two rooms had been empty off her mind. "So, how did the camp go this morning? Tucker and the girls have been holed up in the girls' bedroom since he got back. I haven't had a chance to talk with him."

"Yeah, I saw the note taped to the girls' door. *Keep out. Private meeting.* It sounds like they mean business." Luke smiled.

"I saw that. I wonder what they're up to? I hope they're not planning Tucker's future as a rodeo star." Although Meg was grateful Tucker's preoccupation with the mutton busting had made him happier, she had prayed that once the two-week camp ended, Tucker's mind would move past the rodeo.

"I don't think you have to worry about that. Tucker did have a great time today. He seemed to enjoy the camp. He even met some new friends, but on the way home, he talked more about Rocky and the two of us training the dog than he did about any of the sheep."

This was the first Meg had heard about Luke offering to help train Rocky. Since they had welcomed the dog into their home, she had worried how she'd find the time. "That's nice of you. It's been a long time since I've trained a puppy, so I appreciate any help you can give."

Down the hall, the click of a door lock sounded. Feet thundered toward the guest room.

"We're starving." Tilly rubbed her stomach. "What's for lunch?"

Meg had been so busy going over patient files this morning she hadn't even thought about lunch. With Luke being the only guest, he'd told her she didn't need to worry about feeding him on Saturday or Sunday. "I could make us some grilled cheese. How does that sound?"

Tucker groaned. "We just had that."

Tia nodded.

Meg placed her hands on her hips. "Well, do you have any suggestions?"

The children took turns looking at one another.

"Let's go on a picnic!" Tilly shouted. "We can get some of Mrs. Buser's good fried chicken."

"Yeah, it's the best. We can take it down to the pond," Tucker suggested.

Meg glanced at her watch. "I guess I can run into town and pick up the chicken."

The children all cheered in delight.

Tucker spun on his heel. "I'm going to bring my fishing pole. And I'll get Daddy's pole. Cowboy Luke can fish with me. It'll be awesome!"

Tia slid closer to her brother. "Daddy never liked anyone to use his fishing gear."

Tucker's face grew red. "Well, he's not here, but Cowboy Luke is, and he might want to fish." Tucker looked up to Luke. "Do you think it would be okay?"

Meg noticed Luke directing his attention to her for an answer. It was obvious the children wanted to include Luke in the picnic. She didn't want to disappoint them. "I'm sure your daddy would be fine with Mr. Luke borrowing the fishing rod."

Tucker did a double fist pump. "Me and Cowboy Luke can also show you guys what we've taught Rocky so far."

"I can't wait!" Tilly cried out.

"Come on, girls." Tucker motioned for his sisters. "Let's go get the fishing poles and the blankets that Mommy and Daddy used to bring when we went on a picnic."

The children raced from the room. Rocky followed behind, his toenails scratching against the hardwood floor.

"You don't think—"

Meg looked at Luke and raised her right brow. "What were you going to say?"

"Nothing. It's silly."

"Come on. Tell me what you were thinking."

"I was just wondering if this could all be a part of the kids' plan to get us together. They were just holed up in the bedroom with a sign on the door for us to keep out." One corner of his mouth twisted into a smile.

Meg's cheeks warmed. "No. I put a stop to those plans. They're just excited. What child doesn't like a picnic? I'm sure it's been a while since they've enjoyed a day at the pond." Meg was ashamed to admit she had never thought of having a picnic with the children. There was always so much to do. Her days simply got away from her.

"Yeah, you're probably right." Luke moved toward the door, then stopped and turned. "Why don't I go pick up the chicken?"

"That would be a great help. While you're gone, I can pack up the other things."

"Do you need me to shop at the store for anything else?" Luke offered.

"I think we're good. Thank you, though. I'll pack some drinks and chips. I made a fresh batch of brownies last night."

"Yum. You always made the best brownies. They were always extra gooey." Luke winked and headed out the door.

Meg looked around the room. She was thankful for the hard work Luke and his friends had put into getting the B&B up and running so quickly. She couldn't ignore the fact that if Luke hadn't come back to town, the rooms would have stayed empty for much longer. Perhaps even permanently. She would never have been able to afford the cost of the repairs.

Her stomach fluttered with mixed emotions. Was Luke right? Were the kids trying to play matchmaker? There was a time when she'd been excited by the idea of building a future with Luke. Raising a family and growing old together had been her dream.

Even lately, especially during the car ride home from Connor's house after picking up Rocky, thoughts of them giving the children the stability of family forced their way into her mind, but she fought hard to keep them at bay.

Luke had made his choice years ago.

No matter what feelings were bubbling in her heart, she needed to remind herself that falling for a cowboy meant nothing but trouble.

Luke guided his truck into an open parking spot in front of Buser's General Store. Fond memories of him and Meg as kids flooded his mind—visiting Buser's to share an ice cream float or just to hang out together provided him with comfort.

Countless times he'd wanted to open up to Meg and share with her how his parents had never wanted him, explain how that made him feel, but he could never get up the courage. He didn't want her to think of him as weak, so he kept his feelings locked away.

But all that changed on the day he sat down and wrote her the letter to try and explain. He'd wanted to give her a better understanding of why he had to leave her. Sadly, it was now obvious to Luke that his words on the page didn't seem to ease Meg's anger about his departure. In fact, any time he mentioned the letter since his return, she had abruptly changed the subject.

Luke unfastened his seat belt and exited the truck. A stiff breeze blew against his face. Down the sidewalk, he spotted three boys standing in a cluster. They whispered and looked in his direction.

The taller of the three young boys motioned to the others as he approached Luke. The boy's cheeks blushed. "You're the guy who left here and became the rodeo star, aren't you? I watched you compete last month on television."

The other two boys joined their friend. Their eyes bulged as they stared up at Luke.

"I'm Luke Beckett. And yes, I'm a professional bull rider." Luke stuck his hands into his back jeans pockets.

"I can't believe you've come back to Whispering Slopes," the same boy remarked. "Shouldn't you be getting ready for the big competition next month in Castle Rock?"

So much for keeping a low profile. But Luke could never turn away a young fan. He had some friends who never paid attention to the young people who admired them, only acknowledging the young, pretty women. That had never been Luke's style.

Besides, there was only one woman he had eyes for. But had Meg ever truly cared about him? Had his father been right?

"I'm here resting up before I head back to Colorado." Maybe sooner than he had planned. He scanned the group. "So, are all of you rodeo fans?"

They nodded, and the youngest spoke first. "When I grow up, I'm going to be a cowboy, too. I recently watched a mutton busting competition on television. It was awesome. My dad rode bulls when he was young, but then he met my mom and she made him stop. At least that's what he told me."

Luke smiled. If only he'd done the same. Who knew, by now he and Meg could have had a couple of children of their own. "Mutton busting is the best place to start."

"That's what my dad told me."

"We don't want to be pests, but could we have your autograph?" the older boy asked. He removed his baseball cap and passed it to Luke. "You can sign this. It's better than a piece of paper."

The youngest boy frowned. "But I don't have a hat for him to sign—all of mine are at home."

"Don't worry. I was just going into the store to pick up some things." Luke pointed to the door. "I'm sure we can borrow a pen and paper from Mrs. Buser." Luke pulled the door open, and the three kids filed inside.

"Luke—what a nice surprise." Mrs. Buser rounded the counter and buzzed across the room toward Luke, making adjustments to the gray bun perched on the back of her head. Despite her age, she was a bundle of energy. "I see you brought some friends. Hello, boys."

"Hi, Mrs. Buser," the boys replied in unison.

"We need some pen and paper for autographs. Mr. Beckett is a popular rodeo star," the younger boy announced.

Mrs. Buser smiled at the boy and patted him on the arm. "I'm well aware of our famous former resident. I knew him when he was your age. Let me get you a permanent marker and paper." She scurried off into the back room while the boys fired off questions.

"Does it hurt when you get thrown off?" the little one asked.

"Of course it does, but what about when he gets stomped on by the bull? I'm sure that hurts," the middle boy concluded.

Luke enjoyed their enthusiasm. "I guess after a while you get used to it, but I am getting older, so I have to be careful." Over the past year, Luke had debated when he would call it quits and announce his retirement. He was older than a lot of the other guys, but he wasn't sure he was ready to give up the rodeo life. Who would he be if he wasn't winning awards and being recognized by strangers on the street?

"Here you go." Mrs. Buser returned to the group and handed Luke a black marker and some paper.

"Let me sign this for you." Luke put the pen to the hat given to him outside.

"Oh, man. I wish I would have worn a hat today." The little boy scuffed his foot into the hardwood floor.

Luke scanned the store and spotted a shelf lined with various baseball hats in different colors. "Why don't you guys pick out a hat over there." He pointed. "I'll buy them for you."

"Wow! Cool!" The two boys ran off to make their selection.

Luke turned to the young man. "What's your name?"

"It's Benjamin, but everybody calls me Ben."

Luke signed the hat and handed it back to Ben. "Are you interested in becoming a bull rider one day?"

Ben nodded. "I am, but my parents want me to go to college. I've competed a few times. I think I'm pretty good, but my mom is afraid I'll get hurt. She worries too much."

Luke wasn't about to give the boy any ideas that rodeo life was a dream come true. Of course, he'd been blessed with a lucrative career, but it was tough. Not everyone was cut out for the life. If Luke had had a different relationship with his parents, he might have never taken that road.

"Well, you still have a few years to think about it. You can keep competing and developing your skills until it's time to make a decision."

"Yeah, that's what I thought. Maybe by then, my mom will find something else to worry about." He laughed.

The two boys sprinted back toward Luke, each holding a different colored hat. The youngest passed his to Luke first. "My name is James, but everyone calls me Jamie."

Luke took the white hat and signed it before passing it back to Jamie. "Here you go, buddy."

The redhead with a face dotted with freckles stepped forward. "My name is Tommy."

Luke repeated the gesture. "Okay, I guess you guys are all set."

"Thanks a lot for the signature and their hats." Ben placed his cap back on his head.

"Yeah, thanks," the other boys replied.

"I'll make sure I watch your next competition on

TV." Ben extended his hand and gave Luke a firm shake.

"Thanks a lot. I appreciate it. Take care."

The three children headed out the door chattering about meeting the big rodeo star.

"That was nice of you to do that for them." Mrs. Buser smiled. "Now, how can I help you?"

Luke passed the paper and pen over to Mrs. Buser. "Thanks for this. I wanted to pick up some of your famous fried chicken. I'll need enough to feed three ravenous kids and two adults."

"Oh, I see." She winked. "So, it is true?" The woman clasped her hands together and placed them against her chest.

"What would that be?" Luke asked, even though he could take a wild guess at what she was referring to.

"That you and Meg are back together again. The town has been buzzing about it."

Meg was right—the story had gotten way out of control. "I hate to disappoint you, but that's a silly rumor. Tia and Tilly told a couple of friends. You know how it is in a small town. The story got caught up like a kite with a broken string." Luke watched as disappointment washed over Mrs. Buser's face.

She placed her wrinkled hand to her cheek. "Oh, how sad. Those poor little girls. To dream up such a story with hopes of having a family again. That just breaks my heart."

It was sad. Luke couldn't imagine how their parents could have walked out on their beautiful children. But not knowing the burdens they may have been carrying, he couldn't pass judgment. "Meg is doing the best she can to make a home for them."

"I know she's trying hard. I just want her to have

everything she'd ever dreamed of having. I remember when she was a little girl and she would come into the store with her mother, she'd pretend she was grocery shopping for her family. Three boys, three girls and a dog had all been part of her dream. I'm afraid that will never come true for her. The poor girl hasn't had a date since she's come back to Whispering Slopes."

Luke had been curious about Meg's relationship status. Had she been in any serious relationships since he left? Of course, having three children to care for and two businesses would not leave her much time for a quiet dinner out with grown-ups. "I guess in a small town like this there aren't a lot of available men."

"Well, you're available—aren't you?" Her brow raised.

Luke's heart hadn't been available to anyone but Meg. Unfortunately, she didn't feel the same way. If she had, she wouldn't have ignored the letter. The Meg he'd known and loved would have called or made some attempt to let him know his parents were wrong. "It's complicated."

Mrs. Buser rested her hand on Luke's arm. "Love is never complicated when you follow your heart. A closed heart will lead to a limited life."

The bell over the front door rang, and two children ran inside the store and straight to Mrs. Buser. "Hi, Mrs. Buser! Mommy brought us in to pick up the birthday cake you baked for Daddy." The kids danced a circle around the woman.

Luke's heart ached as he watched the joy the children demonstrated in the act of buying a cake for their father. He hoped the man knew how blessed he was to have children who loved him so deeply.

"I just finished putting the icing on the cake." Mrs.

Buser turned to Luke. "Let me take care of them, and I'll put your chicken in the oven for a couple of minutes. I remember you liked it extra crispy."

"Sure, take your time." Luke smiled at the children's mother and headed down the aisle lined with pet food. His eyes zeroed in on a bag of dog treats—perfect to use to train Rocky. He took the item off the shelf, along with a longer leash, and continued to meander through the store.

A floral aroma hijacked his attention as he turned down the next aisle. He looked around and spotted a display filled with colorful wildflower bouquets. Meg's favorite. Exactly like the flowers he'd given her on her sweet sixteenth birthday. He studied the arrangement. Memories rushed through his mind. His heart told him to buy as many bouquets as he could hold in his hands, but his head won out. Things were different now. She no longer loved him…and maybe she never had.

Chapter Thirteen

"Why do you keep changing your clothes, Aunt Meg?" Tilly wandered through the open door of Meg's bedroom and pointed to the heap of clothing in the middle of the sleigh bed.

Meg's face warmed. Busted. For some unknown reason after Luke left to pick up the chicken, she'd been on an endless search through her closet for the perfect outfit to wear to their picnic. But why? It wasn't like this was a date. She and Luke were doing this for the children. "I thought it would be too warm to wear what I had on earlier."

Tilly scratched her head. "But you were wearing a short-sleeved shirt when I saw you before. Now you've got on a heavy sweater." The child moved closer and ran her hand across Meg's back. "It's so soft. It looks really pretty on you."

Meg turned, bent down and wrapped her arms around her niece. "Thank you. And you're right. I don't know what I was thinking."

"Maybe you want to look extra special for Cowboy Luke."

No. That couldn't be the reason. "I never know what to wear this time of the year."

"You should keep that sweater on for your date."

Meg's back stiffened. "Remember what I told you and your sister. Mr. Luke and I aren't dating. We have no plans in the future to date."

Tilly's lip quivered.

"Oh, sweetie. I didn't mean to snap. I just don't want you and your sister to get your hopes up and then be disappointed when Mr. Luke has to return to Colorado."

"But why does he have to go? He can be a famous cowboy here. I like having him around." Tilly twirled a piece of her hair around her finger.

Meg wasn't surprised the children had become attached to Luke. It was a normal response, but she needed to protect them and make sure they understood he was only visiting Whispering Slopes. "Why don't we just focus on having a good time today and not worry about what the future might bring?"

Tilly listened to her aunt. "That's what we learned about in Bible school last summer, that worry is a waste of time."

Tires crunched on the gravel driveway outside the front of the house. Luke. Her heartbeat accelerated while her stomach turned flip-flops. Why was she feeling this way? It was silly to have this kind of reaction to Luke.

"Cowboy Luke is back. Let's go!" Tilly rocketed out of the room.

Something stirred deep in her stomach. A picnic with Luke could only bring up old memories that were better left buried. Determined to stay strong, Meg inhaled a calming breath and willed herself to follow her advice and not worry. She reached for the picnic basket and headed outside.

* * *

With the bucket of chicken practically empty, Meg leaned back on her elbows with her legs extended in front of her along the grassy bank. "Every time I come down here, I wonder why I don't do it more often."

Luke plucked a piece of grass and stuck it between his teeth. "I can think of three reasons." He pointed to the children at the edge of the pond. Tucker held his fishing rod while the girls dug in the ground for worms.

"You're right. The kids keep me pretty busy. But I'm thankful I've been able to have this time to get to know them better. When I first came home, I'll admit I had some resentment toward my sister. It wasn't easy to give up my practice in Richmond or what I wanted at the time. I loved my practice and the patients."

Luke leaned closer. "And now?"

"I wouldn't trade a second of it for the world. These kids have taught me so much in the past year." Meg had always known she wanted children, but until she'd stepped into the role as caregiver, she'd never realized how life changing parenthood would be.

"So, tell me about your life in Richmond. Did you have a lot of friends?" Luke kept his focus off her and out onto the water.

Meg bit down on her lip to keep from smiling. She knew what he was really asking. "Do you mean male friends?"

He laughed. "Was I that obvious?"

When Meg moved to Richmond, all her time and energy went into building a successful practice. She worked long hours but loved every minute of it.

"Aunt Meg!" The children raced up the bank with Tucker leading the pack. Rocky was leashed and struggled to keep up the pace.

Tucker could barely catch his breath. "Tilly and Tia are getting tired of watching me fish. Can we take Rocky for a walk? We promise we'll stay on the path."

The children knew the trail. The first six months after Meg arrived, she never let them venture out without her. "Okay, but don't go past the stone fencing." She had walked that portion of the trail several times while the kids were at school. The terrain was rough and much too steep for children.

"Yay!" the triplets cheered.

"Don't be gone too long—we still haven't had our dessert," Meg added.

Luke cupped his hands over the sides of his mouth as the children trekked down the path. "And make sure you keep Rocky on the leash, Tucker."

"I will," Tucker yelled over his shoulder.

Meg watched as the children disappeared down the tree-lined trail.

Luke turned to Meg. "What's beyond the stone fence?"

"The river isn't too far. We never go past that area when we go for a hike. They know it can be dangerous. I trust Tucker to be mindful of that. He can be quite protective over his sisters."

Once the children were out of sight, Luke cleared his throat. "So, about all your boyfriends back in Richmond?" He grinned.

Meg playfully slapped her hand on top of his arm. She had hoped he'd gotten off that topic. It was not something she was comfortable talking about with him. "I never said anything about having boy*friends* in Richmond." She emphasized the plural of friends to make a point.

"Oh, so was there one special boy?" He nudged his shoulder against hers.

Luke had been the only one who mattered in her life. Once that ended and her heart was broken, Meg had no desire to give love another try. "No, there wasn't." Meg fingered her necklace. "Can we change the subject? I don't feel comfortable talking about this."

"Sure, I'm sorry. I wasn't trying to pry into your personal life." Luke rubbed the back of his neck and tilted his head from one side and then to the other.

"Is your neck bothering you today?" During their last session, Meg had given Luke a few more exercises to add to his daily routine. Perhaps he'd overdone it.

"It's feeling better than it was before I even got injured." Luke laughed. "Your exercises have worked magic. I feel like I have the neck of a twenty-year-old."

Meg was relieved. The sooner Luke was healed, the sooner he could return to Colorado. That had been his plan. So why the sick feeling in the pit of her stomach? It's what she'd wanted all along. For him to leave town as soon as possible. Wasn't it?

"That's great to hear. By the way, yesterday I was reviewing your file and I noticed that your insurance coverage is nearly maxed out. So, it looks as though we don't have much more time together before you'll be released from my care, unless you want to pay out of pocket. With that in mind, I hope you'll promise to keep up with the exercises."

"I will. You have my word. I do them first thing in the morning, so it's part of my daily routine now."

Meg was relieved to hear this. Often, she would prescribe an exercise plan for her patients, but they wouldn't commit to doing them regularly. The pain would persist, and they'd try to obtain prescriptions to ease it from their physician. Just like her father had chosen to do.

"Aunt Meg! Aunt Meg!"

Meg jumped at Tilly and Tia's bloodcurdling screams. They raced up the hill toward her and Luke. She sprang to her feet. "What's wrong? Where's Tucker?" *The river.* Despite the warmth of the sun, a chill traveled across her skin. Had he gone beyond the stone fence?

"We don't know. That's why we came to get you," Tilly cried out.

"You were supposed to stay in a group." Meg raked her hand through her hair. She never should have allowed them to go off on their own.

"We didn't mean to split up. Tucker was trying to show us the trick he and Cowboy Luke taught Rocky."

Luke joined Meg and looked down at the girls, who were in tears. "Did he take the leash off the dog?"

Tilly kept her eyes focused on the ground and nodded before she yanked hard on Meg's arm. "You have to come help. Rocky ran off, and Tucker went after him."

"Which direction did they go?" Meg scanned the area.

Tia huddled close to her sister. "Tell her, Til."

Tilly lifted her head. "Rocky ran past the stone wall. Tucker kept yelling for him, but he wouldn't come back. Then Tucker told us to stay and wait. We did. We never moved, but then we couldn't hear Tucker yelling for Rocky anymore. We couldn't hear anything except the river."

Tilly wiped her eyes, but the tears continued. "We have to go and find them. If Rocky goes into the water, Tuck will go after him. I just know it!"

"Let me go." Luke gripped Meg's arm.

"But you don't know the trail like I do. You've never seen the stone wall. We'll waste too much time. It's faster if I go," Meg pleaded with Luke.

"You can take me down to the wall and stay with the girls. I'll go from there. You've got to trust me. It's the fastest way," Luke replied. "Girls, come with us, but you'll need to stay with your aunt Meg. Let's go!" Luke sprinted toward the path.

Meg grabbed the girls' hands, and they took off to keep up with Luke. Fallen leaves and twigs from the branches overhead crunched underneath their feet. Earlier, while Meg was deciding on the perfect outfit for the picnic, she'd chosen her open-toed sandals. Now with her feet sliding from side to side, she wished she'd chosen her running shoes.

As the group ventured deeper into the forest, the April sun became veiled by the trees, and the path grew darker. "Don't let go of my hand, girls." Meg squeezed tighter.

"I think I see the stone wall up ahead," Luke called out.

"Yes, that's it." Meg could hardly catch her breath. They had to find Tucker before he ventured close to the river—if he hadn't already.

Luke skidded to a halt. "You all wait here. If you see Tucker, call or text me."

Meg reached into her back pocket. "I left my cell at the house on the charger."

"Then yell as loud as you can. I'll do the same if I find him. Please stay together, and whatever you do, don't leave the spot."

Meg wrapped her arms around her stomach. If anything happened to Tucker, she'd never forgive herself. She was the one who'd given him permission to go off without an adult. "Let's go sit over here and catch our breath." Meg pointed to a fallen tree right off the path. She took a seat. Tilly sat down to her right and Tia to her left.

"What if Cowboy Luke can't find Tucker and Rocky? What happens if it gets dark? He'll never be able to find them then." Tilly nuzzled up against Meg's side.

"Don't worry, sweetie. Mr. Luke will find them." Meg brushed her hand through the child's hair.

A hawk called out overhead.

Meg looked up and silently prayed for Tucker's safety.

Tilly leaned toward her aunt. "Are you scared?"

Meg nodded. "A little, but I just prayed for Tucker to be found safe."

Tilly's brow crinkled. "I pray sometimes, too, but I don't think I talk loud enough."

"Why do you say that, sweetie?"

"Well, I've prayed for my mommy and daddy to come back home, but I don't think God can hear me, because you're still here." Tilly's eyes popped. "Not that I don't want you to stay with us...I just want everyone here together."

Meg reached over and hugged her niece. "I know what you mean."

Minutes later, a muffled voice carried through the trees. "I think I heard something."

The voice sounded once again, only this time there was no mistaking who it was.

"That's Cowboy Luke! What's he saying?" Tilly asked.

Meg stood and moved down the path toward the voice. "Come with me, girls."

"But we're supposed to stay here." Tia, always the rule follower, didn't move.

"It's okay. We can go." Meg motioned to her nieces.

Seconds later, Meg heard the words she'd been praying for. "Luke found him!" she cried out. "Thank You, God."

The girls cheered and danced in a circle, delighted their brother was safe.

The sound of Rocky barking grew closer. Meg spotted Luke walking toward them with Tucker secure in his arms. Her heart squeezed. Tucker clung tight to Luke as if his life depended on it. Meg reached out for Tucker, but he remained in place and buried his face into Luke's shoulder.

"He thinks you're angry at him," Luke whispered.

"Oh sweetie, I'm not mad. I was worried. But you're safe now. That's all that matters."

Tucker raised his head. His eyes were red and swollen from tears. "I took the leash off Rocky. I know I wasn't supposed to, but I wanted to show the girls what he could do."

Meg patted his arm. "It's okay."

"But he ran away from me." Tucker sniffled. "Just like Mommy and Daddy…and just like Cowboy Luke will. Why does everyone leave me?" Tucker whimpered and once again nuzzled his face against Luke's shoulder. "I don't want you to leave me."

Meg and Luke's eyes connected, and he shook his head. She remained silent, but it was obvious Luke knew exactly what she was thinking. Meg couldn't allow this attachment to grow any stronger. The sooner Luke returned to Colorado, the better it would be for everyone involved. That's what her head kept shouting, but she would have to get her heart into agreement.

* * *

"Could you have the bouncy house delivered before eight o'clock next Saturday morning? I have four ponies being delivered at eight thirty." Early Tuesday morning, Luke paced the front porch of the bed-and-breakfast. He scanned his long to-do list on his phone. Would ten days be enough time to take care of all the arrangements? "Seven forty-five? Well, that's even better. Thanks, buddy, I owe you." He ended the call with George, an old rodeo friend, and gazed over the countryside. A calmness took hold. No matter how far away he lived, Whispering Slopes would always be home.

"A bouncy house?" Meg pushed the screen door open and stepped out onto the porch.

"Sure, all the kids love them."

Meg laughed. "I know children like them. I just wondered how you knew this."

"You might be surprised by some of the things that I know, especially when it comes to kids. One of my longtime dreams, once I'm retired, is to open a rodeo camp for children."

Luke's breath caught in his throat. He had never shared his dream with anyone before. He hadn't realized until now how much he missed sharing things with Meg. If only she had called him to acknowledge his letter. In it, he had promised he would do everything in his power to become successful in order to be a good provider. She would never want for anything. Instead, her silence suggested she believed his parents were right. He would never be good enough for her.

"That sounds like a wonderful dream. Knowing you, you'll make it come true." Meg smiled.

Lately, Luke had another dream attempting to take root—one that included Meg and the children—but he needed to pull that root and toss it into the garbage. She'd made it clear she would never commit to a rodeo life. To be with her, he'd have to give up the one thing that provided him stability. "You know me, if I put my mind to something, I can be pretty stubborn." He laughed.

Meg nodded. "I remember. So, when are you going to let me take a peek at your list, so I can help you out? I do own this place. I can't have you doing everything yourself."

Meg moved in closer. A sweet floral aroma tickled Luke's nose. His focus waned.

"I see you have flyers on your list. I can help you out with that. I'm pretty good on the computer. Once I get them printed, I can have the kids help me pass them out around town. I'm sure Mrs. Buser and the other business owners would be happy to share them with their customers."

Luke liked the idea of working together with Meg. "That's a great idea. Do you think the kids' school would be willing to allow some flyers to be posted?"

"I don't see why not. But why are you focusing so much on attracting children with bouncy houses and ponies? My sister always advertised the B&B as a place for a romantic getaway. A location where couples could escape and leave the children at home with a trusted babysitter."

It hadn't taken Luke long to realize that Meg's sister and her husband had made some careless choices when it came to running their business. "I agree. The place is perfect for a couple to enjoy a weekend getaway, but you need to expand your audience. Not everyone has to stay overnight at the B&B. What about giving some serious thought to hosting weddings, reunions, bridal showers or events for businesses? If you want the place to make a profit, you need to have more options and offer more to the customers." Luke's mind had been racing all night with ideas.

"I get what you're saying, but as I mentioned before, the kind of expansion you're talking about takes money that I don't have."

"My offer to invest in the B&B still stands. I see so much potential here." Luke gazed across the rolling hills. "Look over there. You have the beautiful barn, and it sits empty. The place is huge inside. You could use that as a main focal point to have weddings or corporate banquets. The smaller barn could be used for the horses. You could even get some baby goats, like the ones we saw in Staunton."

Meg shook her head. "I love that you have these great ideas, but all I'm seeing are dollar signs. I can't get in over my head and lose the only home these children have ever known. Plus, you won't be here to help."

What if he was? Would Meg agree to a partnership if he stayed in Whispering Slopes? The chances were pretty slim given her silence over the years. But then again, how could he trust her after pouring his heart out to her and being rejected?

"I understand. But at least promise me you'll consider my offer." He could hire people to help her, but getting her to accept would be another hurdle. "Let's see what kind of turnout we have at the open house and maybe we can make our decision at that point." Luke ran his hand along the back of his neck.

"What's wrong? Are you in pain?" Meg stepped closer.

Luke hadn't wanted to mention it, but with his next

and possibly last appointment scheduled for Friday, he had hoped the pain would subside before then.

"You're still under my care. I need to know what's going on."

"It's just a little tweak."

"What does that mean?" Meg folded her arms across her chest.

"I think I had a minor setback. I'll be fine in a day or two." Maybe he should have told her when it had first happened. The last thing he wanted was for her to think he was keeping secrets as her father had done. "Don't worry. I'm not going to take the pain medication."

Meg's eyebrow arched.

She didn't believe him. "I can't. I flushed the pills down the toilet when you first questioned me about them. I know how you feel about them."

"I knew you shouldn't have been working on the drywall project. I should have hired extra men to take care of it."

"That wasn't the cause. It happened on Saturday when I was looking for Tucker on the trail."

Meg's expression went blank.

"I was running and not paying attention. My boot got tangled up in a large root, and I fell. I just kind of jerked my neck a little bit. It's no big deal."

"You should've told me when this happened. I could have helped so the pain wouldn't have gotten worse."

"I thought this would take more than one session to get me back on track. You said it yourself—my insurance is only allowing for one more treatment." That was a moot point. Luke had plenty of money to pay for as many sessions as he needed, but Meg would probably rather he seek another therapist once he went back to Colorado.

Meg frowned. "Do you think all I care about is whether the insurance company compensates me? Your well-being is more important to me than the money."

The look she gave him caused his pulse to surge. Another reason he needed to forget any thoughts about staying in Whispering Slopes and get out of town sooner rather than later. "I appreciate that. I'm sure I'll be fine in a few days."

"Maybe so, but I still would like to evaluate you to see what's going on. I know you had your last appointment scheduled for this Friday, but why don't you pop in tomorrow around the noon hour? I can do a quick evaluation and maybe give you some additional exercises."

Meg wasn't going to take no for an answer. "I don't want to interfere with your lunch break."

"Don't worry about that. I have an appointment at eleven o'clock, but after that, my schedule is open until two."

"Then I'll bring us something to eat. We can make it a working lunch and maybe take care of the flyers."

"You really think this open house idea is going to be the answer to my problems, don't you?"

"I do. I really do." The open house and a lot of prayers. That was Luke's plan.

His cell phone rang. He slipped it from his back pocket and glanced at the screen. Reed. His pulse accelerated. He tapped the button, sending the call into voice mail and placed the phone back in his pocket. He felt Meg's eyes lasered on him.

"An old girlfriend?" Meg half-smiled.

"No, it's nothing like that."

"Is something wrong?"

"It's just something I'm not quite ready to deal with yet."

Reed was waiting for an answer. Normally this was not how Luke dealt with things. He preferred to face things head-on rather than ignore the issue and hope it went away. Reed was only looking out for his best interest.

This was his career on the line, so why wasn't he giving his agent the green light to go ahead with the commercial? He glanced in Meg's direction. His heart squeezed. Were Meg and the children the reason? If so, that could only mean trouble.

Chapter Fourteen

Thursday afternoon, Meg headed to the parking lot at Whispering Slopes K-12 and climbed into her SUV. With the flyers for the reopening delivered to the school secretary for distribution, she decided to run a couple more errands. Miss Mattie was working today, so she could greet the children when they got off the bus. Meg glanced at her list on the passenger seat before easing her foot on the accelerator.

Five minutes later she pulled in front of the post office. Once inside, she used a thumbtack to post one of the flyers to the public bulletin board and headed toward her box to pick up her mail.

Meg slid the key into the lock and opened the door. What in the world? The box was stuffed with piles of envelopes. But how? It had only been a few days since her last pickup. Sorting through the stack, she was relieved to see most of the mail was junk advertisements. Her nerves got the best of her when she spotted an envelope from the bank that held the first and second mortgages on the B&B. This couldn't be good. She debated whether to open it now or wait until she got home. With a few more errands to run, she stuffed the mail into her tote bag. The bank could wait.

Ten minutes into the drive, the correspondence continued to wear on her mind. *It's probably just a solicitation of some kind.* But given her sister's poor money management skills, Meg was afraid it could be something more serious.

Meg pulled her SUV in front of the house and parked. Eyeing the tote, she contemplated leaving it in her car. She was tired and didn't feel like dealing with another problem today, but she knew if she didn't open the letter before going to bed, she'd just stare at the ceiling and think about it all night. She snatched the bag and headed inside the house.

"Here, let me help you with those." Miss Mattie hustled toward Meg as she entered the kitchen with arms full of grocery bags. Her tote loaded with mail and flyers hung off her shoulder.

"Thank you. I appreciate it. My arm is about to break." Once relieved of the load, Meg shook her right hand. "I picked up the ingredients you said you needed for the cookies you plan to bake for the open house. I can't believe it's less than ten days away. I feel like I'm going to run out of time."

"Relax, we'll get everything done. With me doing the baking early and freezing the cookies, I'll be able to work on whatever project you and Mr. Beckett have for me. Besides, the entire town is available to help you with anything else you need." Miss Mattie removed a sack of flour from the bag.

"You're right about that. People have been flooding to my office in town offering their services. Everyone has been so helpful—yourself included. Juggling work, the children and the B&B would be impossible without you. Speaking of, where are the children? Hopefully they're upstairs working on their homework."

"Actually, they're already finished."

Meg stared up at the ceiling. "Really? They certainly are quiet for kids who finished early."

"I thought the same, so I went up to check on them. They said they were working on their secret project."

Meg began to unload another grocery bag. "Any idea what that might be?"

"They're planning to cook you and Mr. Beckett a special dinner. They are determined to get you two together. I can't say that I blame them." She winked.

Meg dropped the loaf of bread in her hands. "Not you, too. I've tried to explain to the kids there is no future for Luke and me, but they don't seem to understand."

Miss Mattie stepped closer. "I don't want to intrude on your life, but you're like a daughter to me. I wondered if you would explain to me why you can't see that the Lord has brought Luke back into your life for a reason. You two are meant to be together."

"I'm not sure I agree with that. Luke made his decision to end our relationship a long time ago. It's all in the past."

"But, dear, people do make mistakes. Perhaps it's time for you to forgive him."

Meg had made her fair share of mistakes in her life, but she couldn't risk having her heart broken again. Getting involved with a cowboy was too risky. Her mother's first marriage was proof of that. Maybe she could forgive him, but she would never forget the pain he'd caused her. "Once I finish here, I better run upstairs and put an end to the dinner planning."

"But they were so excited. It was really cute. They

even recruited me to help with the cooking." Miss Mattie dipped her chin.

"Don't tell me you agreed. You're supposed to be on my side." Meg shook her head. "So, when is this surprise dinner supposed to take place?"

"Tomorrow evening—but you didn't hear from me." Miss Mattie untied the apron from her thick waist and flung it over the back of the kitchen chair. "I'm going to run upstairs and put the sheets on the bed in the hawk's nest room. If you need anything, just yell."

"But the furniture hasn't been put back in place."

"It's taken care of," Miss Mattie called out over her shoulder as she headed toward the stairs. "About an hour before you came home, Luke and two of his rodeo buddies brought all the furniture back up from the barn. It looks nice." Miss Mattie turned and scurried upstairs.

It seemed every time Meg turned around, Luke was doing something to try and make her life easier. And with each effort, he was softening her heart.

The screen door slammed and pulled Meg from her thoughts. She moved toward the sink to wash the potatoes and get them ready to be peeled for dinner tonight.

A soft knock on the wall sounded. "Need any help?"

Meg whirled around and locked eyes with Luke. He stood in the doorway of the kitchen with his hands in the front pockets of his jeans. Her breath caught in her throat for a moment when she realized how much he looked and acted like the same Luke she'd fallen in love with. It felt like a lifetime ago.

"If you feel like peeling potatoes for the potato salad, pull up a chair." She smiled.

"Oh, before I forget. Do you have any more of the flyers we printed? I had a few more places around town in mind."

Meg dried her hand on the dish towel. "I've got some in my bag." She grabbed the oversize tote off the counter and dug inside. She pulled out the flyers, and two pieces of the mail fell to the floor.

"Here, let me get it." Luke bent down, picked up the envelopes and passed them to her.

Meg's pulse ticked up when she spotted the return address label—the bank correspondence. She'd almost forgotten about it.

"You okay?"

"That piece of mail. It's from the bank. It's kind of silly, but I'm scared to open it." She placed the letters on the counter.

"Maybe it's just junk. I get solicitations like that all the time through the mail."

Meg shook her head. "I don't think so. I've never received anything from them. This is the bank that holds the mortgages on the B&B. I recently found some other correspondence my sister had stuffed away—all unopened. I still haven't had a chance to go through it all." She couldn't put it off any longer. "I guess I might as well open it. Maybe you're right. They could be soliciting a new product." Meg grabbed a butter knife from the drawer and ran it along the envelope. As she read the words, her hands began to shake.

"What's wrong?"

"The ten-year rate my sister had on the first mortgage is expiring. Look at the new rate and payment." She handed the paper to Luke.

"Oh boy. That's a big hike."

"And one I can't afford. I'm already up to my eyeballs with unpaid bills. Even if I booked all three rooms solid for the next year, it would have barely kept me afloat. But this—it will bankrupt me." She folded the paper and shoved it back into her bag.

"You okay?" Luke rested his hand on her arm.

"I'm afraid it might be time to talk with the children. I never wanted to break my promise to my sister, but I need to let the kids know there's a chance we might have to sell the B&B and move."

"Are you sure you want to do that now?"

Meg paced the floor. "I can't have them blindsided at the last minute when they see a for-sale sign in the yard."

"It might not come to that. I have an idea if you care to hear it."

"If you're going to bring up investing in the B&B, you're wasting your breath. I've thought about it—a lot. And given our history, I don't think it's a good idea." Meg's thoughts whirled in her head. Accepting Luke's help would be an easy solution. It could allow her to keep the promise she'd made to her sister. But was it that easy? Was it worth the risk?

"I wasn't going to mention it again. I know, once I leave Whispering Slopes, you don't want to have any ties with me. But what do you think about having a fundraiser along with the grand reopening?"

"What? But there's not enough time to plan something like that."

"It will be tight, but I think it can be done. I'll handle all the logistics. I only need you to give me the green light."

Meg could see the determination in Luke's eyes. He wasn't going to let this go. "First I need to know what you have in mind."

"Promise me you'll hear me out before you say no."

Meg nodded.

"We'll host a rodeo. It's a surefire way to draw in a big crowd. We can charge twenty-five dollars per adult and kids will be free."

Meg's head started to pound. "We've been down this road before. You know where I stand on this."

"I know. But it will be a great way to raise a lot of cash fast. You'll be able to pay off all the debt your sister racked up before she left. Fans will come from all over, not just here in Whispering Slopes." Luke pleaded his case.

"I don't mean to sound rude, and I know how popular you are, but do you really think people will come just for you?"

Luke laughed. "They probably wouldn't. That's why I reached out to all of my old rodeo buddies in the surrounding areas. I've already gotten ten to commit."

"So, you contacted your friends before running it by me first. It sounds like you didn't need a green light." Meg leaned against the counter and crossed her arms. She had to admit, it did sound like a great idea. But why was it that everything seemed to involve the rodeo?

"I'm sorry. You're right, I should have checked with you, but to be honest, I got so excited by the idea, I couldn't wait. I came up with the plan when I was at the camp with Tucker. I knew my friends would step up to the plate and offer to help. They're just as excited as I am about the event. Now, with the increase in your mortgage payment, it's the perfect solution. Come on… what do you say?"

Meg thought of the promise she'd made to her sister and the welfare of her three beautiful children. Gina had put her trust in Meg to care for her kids when she felt she was no longer able. Maintaining stability in their life had been Meg's mission from the beginning.

It was important to preserve the only home they'd ever known. Could Luke's idea be the answer? At this point, it might be her only hope to dig her way out of debt. "I suppose we'll need to make up some new flyers." Meg smiled and moved back to the sink.

"I think you're right. It's going to be great…I promise. Now let's get to work on dinner. I'm getting hungry." Luke slid a chair closer to the kitchen sink. "Which drawer has the potato peeler?"

"I'll get it for you." Meg turned off the water and dried her hands on the dish towel before moving toward the drawers in the center island. She fingered through the utensils. Once she got her hands on what she was looking for, she passed it over to Luke. "Here you go." Their fingers brushed, triggering a warmth that made her hand tingle.

When their eyes connected, Luke continued to stare at her. Her shoulders tightened. "Is something wrong?"

Luke shook his head as though he was trying to wake himself up. "I'm sorry. I think I was having a flashback to our high school days."

Meg stepped back toward the sink. She wasn't the only one thinking about their past. This wasn't a good thing. *Stay in the present. Don't look back.* "By the way, thank you so much for moving the furniture back into the hawk's nest. I haven't seen it yet, but Miss Mattie said it looks great."

"No problem. Joe and his rodeo buddy came by to lend a hand. I've got a little bit more touch-up painting to do in the eagle's nest today. Once that's done, we'll get the furniture back in that room tomorrow morning."

"Everything is happening so fast. I can't believe I'm going to be running at full capacity again. Before you came, it seemed like it would be forever until I would be able to offer those rooms. I really appreciate it."

"It was what we agreed to, remember? You provide me with a quiet and low-key place to stay, and I'd get you back up and running at one hundred percent occupancy. By the way, whatever magic you performed on my neck earlier seemed to take care of my setback from the fall the other day."

"I'm glad it's feeling better. If you need one more, it will be on the house since you've gone above and beyond the terms of our initial agreement. We never agreed to you hosting a massive fundraiser that could put me in a position to be debt-free."

The thought of it was mind-boggling. Since Meg had first gained access to the financial records of the B&B, she'd never imagined there would be a time when she could make good on her sister's mistakes and keep her promise.

"I have no doubt that we'll raise enough money to pay off any debt, but don't forget my offer to invest. With the extra money, you could do a lot of the expansions we talked about. We could get this place into a position to provide you with long-term security and stability."

Despite the tempting offer, Meg had to draw the line at the fundraiser. Being business partners with a cowboy wasn't in her future.

Luke waited for a response that never came before he reached into his back pocket. "I almost forgot. I guess you're the person I'm supposed to RSVP to?" He grinned and handed her a red piece of construction paper folded into quarters like a small greeting card.

"What's this?" She opened it and read the invitation written in purple crayon. "What in the world?"

Luke laughed. "I thought you gave up using crayons in grade school."

Meg had no intentions of inviting Luke anywhere. "I didn't make this. Where did you get it?"

"Someone slipped it under the door of my room. I assumed it came from you."

Meg kept a close eye on Luke. "You know I didn't do this, don't you?" She playfully slapped his arm.

"Yes. I'm only joking. The kids are still playing matchmaker. Don't you think it's kind of cute?" Luke pulled his invitation from Meg's hand and slid it back into his pocket. "Did you get one, too?"

"I don't think there is anything cute about it. And no, I haven't seen anything."

"Maybe you should go check your bedroom floor."

Meg had every intention of doing that and more. "I plan to talk to the children about this. Miss Mattie spilled the beans earlier. She's even offered to help them cook the meal. I think she's encouraging them."

Luke picked up a handful of potatoes and placed them on the counter next to his chair. "Don't be too hard on them. I think it's sweet."

"Sweet or not, I think we're sending the wrong message. They're only getting their hopes up. Plus, when you leave, it might stir up their abandonment issues all over again." Who was she trying to kid? It wasn't just the children who would have a difficult time seeing Luke go back to Colorado. But she couldn't admit that to him. It was hard enough admitting it to herself.

"Thanks again for your help, guys." Luke scanned the eagle's nest suite and was pleased. The furniture was all back in place. "The room looks great. I appreciate you both coming over so early this morning."

Joe slipped the screwdriver into his back pocket. "That's not a problem. We know you have a lot of things to do to get ready for the big day, especially since you've decided to host a fundraiser. You're doing a great thing by helping Meg and the kids."

Luke wished Meg would go a step further and allow him to invest in the B&B. His head was flooded with ideas on how to make the place a big attraction while at the same time offering different options from the Black Bear Resort.

"I appreciate your participation. I've been a bit overwhelmed by the response from all the fellas who want to help. Even some of the older cowboys, whose days of getting on a horse have long passed, have agreed to pitch in."

"My riding days aren't quite over, so I'm looking forward to getting back into the ring. I just hope I don't fall on my face while doing a freehand." Joe raised his right arm while pretending to hold on to an imaginary bull with the other.

Luke had no doubt his friend could still hang on longer than most bull riders. Joe had always been a tough competitor. "I'm sure you'll do fine."

"Remember to give me a call if you need help with anything. I've got a lot of free time on my hands since I'm retired." Joe and his son headed out into the hallway.

"I'll do that. Thanks again, guys." He waved.

Luke went back to work painting a second coat on the small area of trim outside the bathroom when his cell phone rang. He pulled the device from his pocket and scanned the screen.

He sighed. Reed's calls were getting more frequent. His agent wanted an answer, but Luke wasn't ready to make any decisions. Without hesitation, he sent the call to voice mail.

He took note of the time and realized he needed to get a move on so he wouldn't be late for his speaking engagement at the kids' school. With that in mind, he decided to head downstairs for a cup of strong, black coffee. He placed the lid back on the can of paint and headed to the dining room, following the aromas of coffee and bacon.

"Good morning, Luke." Miss Mattie stood in the dining room holding a full pot of fresh brew. "I figured the smell would lure you downstairs."

"It sure did." He settled into a chair while she filled his cup. "I've got a busy day, so keep the coffee coming."

Miss Mattie turned to the buffet and placed the pot on the warmer. "I'm sure you're busy getting things ready for the open house and the fundraiser, but make sure to be home in time for dinner tonight." She flashed a smile and gave Luke a wink.

Luke hadn't forgotten. He'd been awake half the night thinking about it. Despite Meg's reservations about the dinner, he was looking forward to some quiet time alone with her. Just the two of them. Like it used to be. He could take those memories with him back to Colorado. "You know I'll be here. Everything will be ready by six o'clock on the dot."

"The children are so excited." She clapped her hands together.

Luke watched Miss Mattie scurry from the room. The two of them had made a good team. Once Luke had learned Miss Mattie was assisting the kids with their matchmaking idea, he'd offered to help, too. The children's plan was ready to put into action. All that was left to do was to wait to see Meg's reaction. He opened up the newspaper left on the table.

"Good morning."

Luke pulled his eyes away from the latest town news and looked up. Meg stood in the doorway. He swallowed hard to push the lump down his throat. Dressed in a fun and flirty yellow dress with a cardigan of the same color covering her shoulders, she looked gorgeous. "Wow, you look great this morning."

Meg fidgeted with the sides of her dress and blushed. She glanced down as if she'd forgotten what she was wearing. "Oh…thank you. It's such a beautiful morning, I felt like wearing something springy." She looked down again. "Do you think I'm overdressed for the office?"

Luke had hoped she had dressed up for the dinner tonight. But that was only wishful thinking. Meg had only agreed to the invitation because she didn't want to upset the children. "No, not at all."

"I have a packed schedule today, and I'll be running short on time. I wasn't sure I'd have time to change before dinner."

Wait. Maybe she *had* taken extra time to pick a special dress and fix her hair perfectly for him.

"I hate to rush."

Nope. She'd done it to save time. Either way, she looked stunning. "Speaking of rushing, I made new flyers for the fundraiser last night. I plan to deliver some around town after I finish with the big Friday surprise at the school this morning. Since the kids have already caught the bus, I suppose it's okay to share with you."

"What's going on?" Meg poured a cup of coffee and settled into the chair across from Luke.

"I'm speaking at the kids' school this morning. I ran into Mrs. Cooper the other day downtown. She said she had asked you to run it by me, but you must have forgotten."

"I did. I'm sorry."

"No worries. Mrs. Cooper spoke with the principal. Nick thought it would be nice if the entire school could listen to my presentation. I'll be in the auditorium at ten thirty, if you're interested."

"Well...I...like I said, I have a busy schedule today. I have appointments into the early part of the afternoon."

Luke reached across the table and placed his hand on top of hers. "Relax. I was only joking. I know you don't like anything that relates to bull riding or the rodeo. I get it."

"I'm sure the kids will love it. It's nice of you to agree to this, especially since you're so busy and you'll be going back to Colorado before you know it." She pulled her hand away and gazed out the window.

Would Meg miss him once he left? More than likely, she was counting the days off on her calendar until he was out of her hair.

But lately, he'd been thinking less about Colorado and more about what was here in Whispering Slopes. The possibility of a life with the only woman he'd ever loved and three children who'd stolen his heart.

Being number one and winning might have made his parents happy, but this was his life, not theirs.

Chapter Fifteen

For the fourth time since she'd returned home from work, Meg changed her clothes. When her last appointment of the day had canceled, she'd found herself with time to spare and too much time to think. After working all day in the special outfit she'd picked out for the evening, it didn't feel quite as special.

Now she questioned whether to wear her hair up or down this evening. She dropped the clips onto the bathroom vanity, opting for down. Why did she care so much what her hair looked like tonight?

She knew why. And it had taken her completely by surprise.

Lately, it had become more difficult to deny the feelings that had rekindled whenever she was around Luke. A part of her wished she could just lock them away, like the letter Luke had written to her. The letter that had remained unread.

Since Luke had returned, he'd asked her about the letter a couple of times, but she'd refused to talk about it. A part of her was ashamed to admit that she had never read beyond the first two sentences, but why? All her dreams had been shattered the day she learned he had left Whispering Slopes. Back then, her teenage heart didn't care about reading something he had been unable to tell her face-to-face. If she had, would it have changed anything?

Meg studied her reflection in the mirror. For a second, she caught a glimpse of that young, brokenhearted teen. Why had she been afraid to read Luke's letter? Slowly, she moved toward the cedar hope chest at the foot of her bed. Constructed by her father before his career-ending injury, the chest had been given to Meg by her mother.

She opened the lid. Only two things had ever been placed inside the dark box—her mother's wedding dress and the diary where Meg had recorded her dreams and desires as a young girl. Tucked away between the yellowing pages and faded black ink was Luke's good-bye letter.

She brushed her hand across the soft brown leather before opening the gold quick-snap closure. Luke's letter broke free from the pages and drifted to the floor. Her heart paused a beat. She picked up the envelope and removed its contents. Meg moved to the side of the bed and sat on the edge. As she read his words, her throat tightened, and she fought to hold back the tears. Luke hadn't left because he'd stopped loving her. He'd left because it was the only way he believed he could be loved.

An hour and a half after reading Luke's letter, Meg had put herself back together. Her modest amount of eye makeup that had ended up running down her cheeks had been wiped clean, much in the same way as the anger she'd held on to for so many years.

Surprise took hold when Meg stepped into the empty

dining room. The dimmer lights were adjusted to low, and the table showed no sign of an impending meal.

"There you are. I was just about ready to come looking for you," Miss Mattie said as she entered the room.

Meg smoothed her hair. "I'm sorry if I'm late. I got a little sidetracked."

Miss Mattie stepped closer and took Meg's hand. "Are you okay, dear? You look like you've been crying."

Washing her face and reapplying her makeup couldn't erase the pain in Meg's eyes or her heart. Thoughts of Luke suffering in silence all those years had overwhelmed her. "Yes. I'm fine. I'm a little confused about the dinner. Did the children finally come to their senses?"

Miss Mattie laughed. "Oh, no. They've been hard at work since they got home from school this afternoon."

No matter how much Meg tried to make it clear to the kids that there was no future for her and Luke, it was as though they knew something she and Luke didn't. "Where are we going to have dinner?"

"I'll show you."

Luke's deep voice sounded from behind her. Meg whirled around, and for a second, she couldn't breathe. Dressed in a crisp white button-up shirt and tan pants, he wore a smile that caused her knees to grow weak.

He moved closer and reached for her hand. Meg caught a whiff of a clean, soapy scent. He never did like to wear cologne. "You smell nice."

Luke smiled. "You look nice. You changed your dress."

After reading Luke's letter, Meg had riffled through her closet for a fifth time in search of the perfect dress for dinner. "I did." Her cheeks warmed.

"Green is my favorite color."

"I remember." When Meg had stepped into her closet for the last time, she knew just the dress she was looking for. Luke always told her that green was her color. He said it brought out the sparkle in her emerald eyes.

Miss Mattie broke the silence that hung in the air. "You two better get going. The children are waiting for you."

Meg looked at the woman. "You haven't told us where we're going."

"I'll show you." Luke locked arms with Meg. "Let's go."

Outside a chorus of tree frogs sounded. The air was still with a hint of warmth.

"Do you need to run back inside for a jacket?" Luke asked as they walked down the porch steps.

Being near Luke triggered a warm and tingling sensation. It brought back memories of the first time he'd put his high school football letterman jacket over her shoulders. "No. I'm fine."

Once they stepped off the gravel driveway, Meg's feet slid in the dewy grass. "I'm glad I wore flats tonight instead of heels."

"I should have warned you." Luke held on a little tighter.

"So, how is it you know where to go and I don't?" Had Luke joined forces with Miss Mattie? Was he in on the execution of this plan?

Luke remained silent. The flashlight from his cell phone kept the path illuminated until they reached the smaller of the two barns.

"We're eating in the barn?" The last time Meg was inside, the space had been filthy. Even without animals, the aroma of past tenants had lingered. "Maybe I should have worn jeans."

Luke smiled and pulled the door open.

Meg released a gasp and cupped her hands over her mouth.

"Come inside," Luke suggested.

Twinkling fairy lights filled the space. "It's so beautiful."

"That's why I knew where to go. Someone had to help the kids hang the lights." Luke winked and guided her to the round oak table with crystal tea lights illuminating the center. Soft music filled the structure.

"So, did the kids install the speaker system by themselves?" Meg gave Luke a questioning eye.

"Connor took care of that for me the other day."

Just what she thought. Luke had been in on the plan. Had it been his idea from the beginning? She couldn't deny it—the thought of Luke cooking up the idea for a romantic dinner had a completely different effect on her now than it would have earlier today.

Luke pulled out a chair for Meg and then slid into a seat across from her. His eyes stayed focused on her as she drank in the romantic atmosphere. "I can't believe this is the same place. It doesn't even look like a barn."

"Good evening."

Meg turned, and her heart melted. Tucker stood beside the table dressed in a dark suit. He held a pitcher of water and what looked like menus underneath his arm. With his formal mannerism, Meg decided to play along. "Good evening to you, sir." She reached for the menus, and Tucker proceeded to fill the water glasses.

"After you've had a chance to look at the menu, the server will be over to take your order." Tucker pulled a small hand towel from his inside pocket on his jacket and wiped the sides of the pitcher before he scurried away.

"Who was that?" Meg laughed and took a sip of

her water. "I've never seen Tucker so serious. Did you write a script for him?" Meg glanced at the menu. Her stomach fluttered when she read the offering. There was only one selection—crab cakes. Her favorite, and the first meal she ever shared with Luke.

"I may have given him a few lines, but the kids are indeed on a mission."

"And what would that be?"

Luke leaned forward with a twinkle in his eyes. "To get us back together."

"What's your motive in all this? You've obviously helped the kids with their plan. What's in it for you?" Did she hope Luke wanted the same as the children, or was it a combination of reading the letter and the romantic atmosphere that was jumbling her thoughts?

Luke picked up his menu. "We can talk after we've had our dinner." He nodded. "It looks like our servers are coming for our order."

Meg peered over her shoulder and spotted Tilly and Tia. They wore their Easter dresses Meg had bought last year. Both had their hair pulled up in tight buns. "They look adorable—so grown-up."

"I wonder if we'll have to tip both of them?" Luke laughed and turned his attention to the menu.

An hour later, Meg leaned back against the chair. "I'm stuffed. One of these days I need to have Miss Mattie teach me some of her secrets in the kitchen."

"She is a terrific cook. Those were the best crab cakes I've ever eaten." Luke rubbed his stomach.

"They always were my favorite." Meg blotted her mouth with the cloth napkin.

"I remember."

"Is that why it was the only choice on the menu?" Meg waited for Luke's response. She wanted it to be the reason. After so many years of believing Luke chose the rodeo life over her, discovering the truth had changed everything. Was this God's plan, like Miss Mattie had said, to bring the two of them back together? Was this their second chance? For the first time since Luke had returned, Meg found herself excited by the thought.

Luke took in a deep breath. Was Meg ready to talk? She hadn't been open to any discussion about their past or the letter since he'd come back to Whispering Slopes. It appeared she was opening the door. Or was it only wishful thinking?

"I have a confession. The dinner was the kids' plan, but once I learned about it, I did have a few motives of my own."

"I'm listening." Meg picked up her coffee cup and took a sip.

"It was my idea to have dinner in the barn instead of at the house. I thought it would be a good way to show you the potential for expanding your business."

"I kind of had a feeling that was your intention. And you know what?" Meg scanned the area. "You were right. Seeing the place transformed has made me realize it is a perfect venue to host an array of functions. I just never saw the potential. You've opened my eyes to a lot of things."

Was Meg finally going to agree to his offer to invest in the B&B? If she did, he could go back to Colorado with peace of mind that she and the children would be financially secure. It might relieve some of the guilt he carried for leaving her.

But where would that leave him? Being secure in his finances hadn't given Luke the stability he longed for. Sure, he could buy anything his heart desired. Do whatever he wanted to do. But the money couldn't buy what he'd wanted his entire life—the stability of a loving family.

"I'm happy to hear that."

"I think I'm ready to accept your offer to help me expand the B&B. If it still stands."

"Of course it does."

"But first, I have a confession of my own." Meg's voice was flat.

Luke straightened his back. "I guess it's my turn to listen."

"The letter you gave me…before you left—I never read it."

Luke had never imagined that was the reason Meg changed the subject whenever he brought up his letter. He assumed the topic was too painful to discuss, or that she was never going to forgive him no matter what he had said. "Why not?"

"When you left, I was so angry at you. You had chosen to be a bull rider over marrying me."

Luke shook his head. "There was so much more behind my decision to leave."

"I know that now, but not then. I wasn't just angry at you. I was hurt. You had betrayed me. Just like my father. You loved bull riding more than me. That was hard for me to accept. I didn't want to hear what you had to say. I wasn't ready. So instead, I stuffed your letter into my diary, where it remained—until tonight." Meg brushed a tear from her face.

"So, you did read it?"

Meg reached across the table and took his hand. "Why didn't you ever tell me you were harboring so much pain?"

A lump formed in Luke's throat. "I was embarrassed.

Or maybe ashamed is a better word. As a kid, it was a hard thing to wrap my head around. My parents never wanted me. They resented me for being born. I had ruined their lives."

Meg allowed her tears to flow freely. "I wish I'd known."

"The day I left, my father and I had a huge fight. He told me I was wrong to think you and I could ever get married. He said I had nothing to offer you but a closet full of worthless trophies." Luke shook his head. "I believed him. Since my parents didn't love me, how could I have expected you to?"

Meg squeezed his hand tighter. It gave him the courage to continue to relive that painful moment.

"I was too upset to come and see you in person, so I wrote the letter and left." He pulled his hand from Meg's and rubbed his face. "I was determined to make something of myself. I had to prove to my parents that I was worthy of their love—of yours."

"Did you? With them?"

"No. But in time my relationship with God grew stronger. I had His love. That was what mattered. It's what gave me the power to start to forgive my parents and to heal some of the wounds. But I don't know if I can put all the blame onto them."

"What do you mean?"

Luke leaned back against the chair. "After my father said I wasn't good enough for you, I started to question your true feelings toward me. I wondered if he was right. When I wrote the letter, I think I used it as a test of your love."

For a moment, Meg remained silent and simply nodded her head. "How is your relationship with them now? Have they accepted responsibility for their actions?"

Luke shook his head. "No. I don't think my father feels any differently toward me. He blames a lot of the problems he and my mother had on me. They're older now, and my mother has dementia."

"I'm sorry your father hasn't realized he was wrong," Meg said.

They shared a quiet moment while Luke grieved for what could have been. A different life, if only his parents had loved him.

"Are you guys finished eating? We're getting a little tired." Tucker broke the silence that hung within the walls of the barn.

Luke had been so focused on the conversation with Meg, he hadn't noticed the children had come into the room.

Miss Mattie scurried to the table. "I'm sorry they interrupted you. They slipped away from me."

Meg's chair screeched along the floor. She stood and hugged each child. "Thank you for everything. It was a perfect evening."

"It would be even more perfect if Cowboy Luke asks you to marry him," Tilly announced before she zipped out of the barn. Her sister and brother followed.

"Out of the mouths of babes," Miss Mattie responded. "Why don't you two go for a little walk around the pond? There's a gorgeous full moon tonight. I'll get everything cleaned up."

"We can't leave you here with all this." Meg glanced down at the table of dirty dishes.

Luke and Miss Mattie exchanged an understanding look. Earlier, Luke had told Miss Mattie that he would handle the cleanup early tomorrow morning since it was her day off, but she'd insisted on taking care of it.

"I'll have this cleared away in no time." Miss Mattie began to load the plates onto the serving cart.

Outside, the full moon provided ample light as Luke and Meg moved down the path toward the pond. Luke offered his hand, and she accepted. Slowly he raised their intertwined fingers to his face and gently brushed his lips against her soft skin. Sweet memories flooded his mind.

Meg turned. Her eyes glistened in the light. "This is nice," she whispered.

It was. There was no denying the feelings Luke still had for Meg and hopefully she had for him. Excitement coursed through his veins as he pictured the two of them making evening strolls part of their daily routine. Stability. Not from awards and accolades, but from a healthy and loving family.

They approached the pond and took a seat on the bench. An Eastern screech owl sounded from a nearby tree. Meg held tightly to his hand and rested her head on his shoulder. They sat in silence. Words weren't necessary. Had their love for each other survived the storm?

Luke gazed out over the stagnant and still water confined within the banks of the pond, the opposite of the Shenandoah River that reached out to new places, constantly flowing and providing new growth. That's what he wanted for his life, not one confined to a rodeo arena. God had used his injury to lead him home to share his life with Meg and the children. But could Meg trust her heart to him a second time? He'd do whatever it took. He had to. Because with Meg at his side, he didn't want to live a pond-like life one second longer.

Chapter Sixteen

"Look, Aunt Meg!" Tucker shouted from across the kitchen, still dressed in his pajamas.

Meg had been going nonstop since her feet hit the floor early Saturday morning. The big day was finally here. She should have been exhausted from all the preparations over the past week, but instead she was energized. Since last Friday evening, she could hardly keep her focus on the reopening of the B&B and the fundraiser that would start in under two hours. Her thoughts had been consumed with Luke and the time they'd been spending together. She could no longer deny her feelings for him.

"What is it, Tuck?" Meg called over her shoulder. She stood at the island and placed the chocolate chunk cookies Miss Mattie had baked onto a large silver platter. These treats would stay inside and be offered to the guests coming through to tour the B&B. Several of Luke's cowboy friends were handling the food to be served outside during the rodeo events.

"I taught Rocky how to sit. Do you want to see?"

Meg wiped her hands on the dishcloth and moved to the far corner of the kitchen. In addition to outside, the space had become the designated spot for Tucker to train Rocky since it was close to the laundry room, where Luke had stored the dog's treats.

Tucker plucked a piece of dried liver from the plastic container. Rocky's eyes followed his every move. With the treat secure in his fist behind his back, Tucker used his other hand to point at the dog. "Okay, Rocky. Do it again and you'll get your treat." The dog's ears perked to attention. "Now, sit." Without a moment of hesitation, the puppy flopped his backside to the hardwood floor. His tail swished across the wood as Tucker fed him the chunk of liver. "Good boy." Tucker patted his head.

Meg clapped her hands together. "That's amazing. Did you teach Rocky to do that all by yourself?"

"Kind of. Cowboy Luke showed me what to do. He said if I kept trying, even when I got frustrated and wanted to give up, Rocky would do it. And he was right. I have a bunch of other tricks I want to teach Rocky. I just wish Cowboy Luke would be around to see them." Tucker's excitement faded.

For a second, Meg's excitement also began to wane. It was true. Since the other night, things seemed to have changed between her and Luke. They were more relaxed and playful around each other. So much so that the other day, after his last therapy session she'd offered off the books, she'd thought he was going to kiss her as he was getting ready to leave. But the mayor had popped into her office without an appointment and put the brakes on the romantic vibe in the air.

She couldn't be upset with the mayor. He'd stopped by to offer his assistance with anything she and Luke might need today.

"Do you think he'll change his mind and stay?"

Tucker's question pulled Meg back into the moment.

Exactly where it should be. She needed to keep her focus on the events of the day. Getting out of debt and having a steady flow of reservations for the newly re-modeled suites was the plan, to uphold her promise to Gina. Yes, she and Luke would be business partners, but she had to accept the fact that might be where their relationship ended.

"Mr. Luke has to go back to his work." Meg glanced at her watch. "As do we. People will be arriving shortly. Why don't you run upstairs and get dressed? I'll have your cereal ready in a couple of minutes, so send your sisters down."

Tucker moved slowly from the room. Rocky followed behind.

Voices sounded from the gathering room. Luke was speaking with Miss Mattie. Despite today being her day off, she had volunteered to come over to help with the food and serving the guests. Meg didn't know what she would do without her. Miss Mattie had been like a mother to her. It was obvious she wanted Luke to stay in Whispering Slopes as much as the children did. If Meg was honest with herself, it's what she wanted, too.

"I can't believe the crowd out there." Luke entered the kitchen dressed in simple straight-leg blue jeans, a long-sleeved button-down shirt, dark brown leather boots and a gently worn cowboy hat. "We haven't even officially opened, but we've almost sold out all the seats."

Meg's pulse picked up. And not just a little. It took off like a rocket. She would be the first to admit she might not like the bull riding profession, but she loved the look, especially on Luke. He was more handsome than she had ever seen him look.

Get a grip, girl.

"It's good that Connor and his friends were able to get their hands on the extra stadium seating."

"Yeah, the place looks great. It's almost identical to an event I attended last month in Wyoming."

Meg considered Luke's expression. His eyes brightened whenever he shared stories about the rodeo and events from his past. It brought him joy. How could she expect him to give that up? Not to mention the financial security it provided for him. Plus, his bull riding buddies were his family. They had all answered his call to help Meg save her business from financial ruin. Maybe rodeo life wasn't so bad.

"I'm truly overwhelmed by the turnout, and by all your cowboy friends who helped put the event together in such a short amount of time. I owe it all to you." Meg turned her head slightly to conceal her emotions.

In two strides, Luke closed the space between them. With his right thumb, he gently wiped away the lone tear that raced down her cheek. "No tears today, unless smiles follow. This is a day to give thanks and to celebrate. There are so many people out there who love and care about you. They believe in you and the B&B. It's time for you to start believing in yourself."

Meg felt Luke's warm breath on her face as he leaned in. His soft lips brushed her own. For a second, she thought it was a dream, but when the familiar muscular arms wrapped tightly around her waist, she knew it was better than any dream she'd ever had. It was real. She was back in Luke Beckett's arms.

A buzz sounded. Luke jumped and stepped back, leaving Meg longing for one more kiss. "I'm sorry. It's my phone." He slipped the device from his back pocket and scanned the screen.

Luke frowned and tapped the phone before putting it

back in its place. The unanswered calls were happening more frequently. Over the past week, Meg couldn't help but wonder if Luke was involved with someone. Was there a woman back in Colorado counting the minutes until his return? "Wrong number?"

Luke shook his head. "No. It's my agent again. I'm ashamed to admit that I've been avoiding his calls."

Meg relaxed her shoulders. It wasn't another woman. "Why don't you want to talk to him? It's not like you to avoid people."

"You're right. I haven't been handling the situation very well. It's just a little complicated."

"I'm here if you want to talk about it," Meg offered.

"He's calling about a commercial deal."

"That sounds exciting…and much safer than riding a bull." Meg had given a lot of thought to Luke returning to competition. Even though his neck seemed to be doing fine, she still worried for his safety.

Luke smiled. "You're for anything that keeps me out of the arena, aren't you?"

"I don't want you to get hurt again. Why wouldn't you want to do the commercial? I've never known you to be camera shy."

"You're right about that, but it's not just a commercial. It's a big deal. Huge, actually. The biggest of my career. It's a series of commercials for a truck manufacturer. They'll be filmed at various locations all over the country. I would be a celebrity representative for the company."

Meg ran her hand down the front of her jeans. "It sounds like you'll be busy jet-setting all over."

Luke nodded. "It would be a big commitment of my time. According to Reed, I would be giving the company the next sixteen months of my life."

The screen door slammed, and the sound of heavy boots hitting the floor filled the room.

"Luke, we need your help outside." Connor stood at the door. "My friend is here with the trailer. We've got to unload the animals."

"Sure, buddy." Luke turned and followed Connor out the door.

A wave of sadness hit Meg. It was happening all over again. There was no way she could compete with a lucrative commercial deal. She'd been foolish to think Luke could be happy staying in tiny Whispering Slopes. He was a cowboy through and through.

Cowboys didn't settle down. They needed to roam free. As much as she tried to convince herself, the writing was on the wall.

For the second time in her life, Luke Beckett was going to break her heart.

After helping to unload the trailer and tending to some last-minute details, Luke stepped out of the barn and spotted several of his bull riding buddies surrounded by a mob of excited fans. Despite the tight schedule of events, the guys were taking the time to sign autographs. That was a good thing.

Luke smiled and gazed out over the grassy field. As far as his eyes could see, there were hundreds of vehicles. Luke never could have imagined such a large turnout.

Even with the success of the fundraiser and the reopening of the B&B, a cloud of dread hovered over his head at the thought of returning to Colorado. If he had a lick of sense, he would have answered his agent's call and told Reed that Meg and the children were more important than any amount of money.

"Cowboy Luke!"

Luke spun around and spotted Tilly and Tia running toward him at top speed with their arms flailing. They looked adorable dressed in matching cowgirl skirts with tiny boots and their hair in braids.

"Will you take us to the barrel racing? I have to see it!" Tilly performed a quick spin, causing her cowboy hat to go flying off her head.

"She thinks that's what she's going to do when she grows up." Tia rolled her eyes under the brim of her hat.

Tilly placed her hand on her hips. "I am. Cowboy Luke said girls can do it. Will you take us...please?"

"Of course. But it won't start for another hour." Luke looked around. "Where's your brother? Doesn't he want to go?"

"He's down at the pond. He was being mean to us, so we left him alone."

"That doesn't sound like Tucker. Maybe I'll walk down and see if he's okay."

Tilly shrugged her shoulders. "Whatever. I'm not going to let him ruin my day. Come on." She motioned for her sister. "Let's go get a hot dog before the barrel racing." The girls took off toward the grill.

Luke headed across the field and down the grassy embankment. Tucker had been doing so much better the past couple of weeks. He'd talked nonstop about the fundraiser and seemed excited about today.

Luke spotted the boy sitting on the ground staring out over the water. Rocky, his new and constant loyal companion, sat by his side.

"Hey, buddy. Do you mind if I take a seat?"

Tucker shrugged his shoulders. Luke took that as a yes. He settled down beside Tucker. "What's up?"

"Nothing."

Okay. This might be more difficult than he'd thought. "How's the training coming along? Have you gotten Rocky to sit for you?"

The puppy's head lifted from the grass at the mention of his name. He looked around and let out a sigh before resting his head back on top of his oversize paws.

"It doesn't matter."

"What do you mean? You've worked hard. Of course it matters."

Tucker picked up a handful of dirt and threw it toward the water. "No, it doesn't!"

Luke took a glance at Tucker. He was biting down on his lip, obviously trying to hold back his tears. "Do you want to tell me what's bothering you?"

"Why do you care? Aunt Meg told me earlier that you're leaving soon."

"But you knew I had to go back to Colorado. Remember? I said we could talk on the phone and maybe you could come out for a visit sometime."

This wasn't good enough for Tucker. And to be honest, Luke wasn't sure it would be good enough for him, either.

"I know, but I've been praying for you to stay. I guess God doesn't listen to me. Just like He didn't when I prayed for Him to bring my mommy and daddy back home."

Luke recalled having some unanswered prayers of his own when he was younger, but he'd later realized he couldn't question God's timing. "Sometimes God has His own plan for our life. We might not always agree or understand, but we have to trust Him and His timing. He always knows what's best for us."

Tucker reached out and scratched the top of Rocky's head. "Maybe me and Rocky can go back to Colorado with you. Since my daddy is never coming back for me. Maybe you can take his place?" He rubbed his eyes.

"I would love for you to come to Colorado, but don't you think your sisters and your aunt Meg would miss you? And I have a feeling you would miss them, too."

"Yeah, maybe a little."

Luke had a feeling Tucker's little emotional melt-down was subsiding…at least for now. He patted Tucker's leg. "Let's go find your sisters. They wanted you to watch the barrel racing with them."

They rose, and Tucker secured the leash around Rocky's collar before they headed up the hill. Once at the top, Luke's stomach rolled over. It couldn't be. He stopped in his tracks.

"What's wrong?" Tucker stopped and followed the direction of Luke's eyes. "Who's that man talking to Aunt Meg?"

Luke hoped he'd been mistaken, but he wasn't. Meg was standing beside one of the grills holding a plate of food and talking to his agent. What in the world was Reed doing here? Tia and Tilly stood by their aunt nib-bling on hot dogs.

As Luke and Tucker approached, Meg turned, her expression solemn.

"Reed—I'm surprised to see you here." Luke's voice shook.

His agent extended his hand. "It's good to see you, too." He forced a laugh. "If you answered your phone, maybe you wouldn't be so surprised. I called earlier from the airport to let you know I was in town." Reed glanced at Meg before turning his focus back on Luke. "Can we go somewhere and talk?"

Luke threw darted glances at Meg and the three chil-dren. His heart hammered against his rib cage. This was exactly where he planned to stay. "We can talk here." His eyes skimmed Meg. "I don't have any secrets."

Reed opened the leather portfolio tucked under his arm. "Since we're running short on time, I thought I'd bring the contract to you so we can go over it before you sign. We don't want to cut it too close to the deadline." He removed the papers and pointed to the nearby picnic tables. "It might be more comfortable if we have a seat over there."

Luke reached for the contract. "That won't be necessary." He held the stack of pages out in front of his extended arms. "I know you've worked hard on this deal. I appreciate it, but I'm not signing."

"Luke!" Meg cried out. "Endorsements bring in the big money."

Luke turned to Meg. "You mean more to me than any amount of money, Meggie." He handed the contract back to Reed.

"Cool!" Tilly cheered.

"Wow!" Tucker added.

"What are you doing, man? Everyone dreams of this kind of offer," Reed stated.

Meg looked at Luke with tears streaming down her face.

"I guess I'm not like everyone," Luke spoke with confidence.

Reed nodded and smiled. "No, you're certainly not. Maybe that's why we're such good friends."

Luke stepped closer to Meg and pulled her into his arms. She smelled like fresh honeysuckle. "You're what I've dreamed of. I promise I won't walk away again." His eyes locked onto Meg. "I did it once, and it was the biggest mistake of my life." He leaned in and brushed his lips against Meg's mouth. "I love you. I want to stay here and share my life with you and the kids. We can have more children, if that's what you want."

Reed patted Luke on his back and walked away. The triplets danced a little jig, cheering and high-fiving each other.

"What do you say? Will you marry me?" Luke held his breath, waiting for her to answer.

Meg wiped her eyes and smiled. "Yes." She closed the space between them and gave him a soft kiss. "I love you, too, Cowboy Luke. I would be honored to become your wife."

Luke stroked his hand across Meg's cheek. It had been a long and difficult journey, but he'd found his way back home and into the arms of the only woman he'd ever loved.

Epilogue

"Triplets! Woo-hoo!" Luke threw his cowboy hat up in the air, swept Meg off her feet and twirled her around the inside of the arena. A cloud of dust kicked up into the air. Luke's laughter carried across the rolling farmland, and the children giggled. A horse grazing in the field whinnied.

"Put me down! I'm getting dizzy." Meg was already light-headed following her doctor's appointment earlier this morning.

Multiples can run in the family, the doctor had told her as she tried to wrap her head around the idea of raising two sets of triplets.

"It's not funny. How will we ever handle six kids, a B&B with a year waiting list for guests and weddings, my busy practice, and the rodeo camp?"

Luke placed Meg back on the ground. He leaned in and moved his warm lips gently onto hers.

Meg's heartbeat pumped faster than she thought possible. The way it always had when Luke kissed her. The way it always would.

"I can think of worse problems to have. Come on, Meggie. We'll manage. We always do."

Luke was right. The good Lord had provided abundant blessings over the past year. They were thankful Meg's sister and brother-in-law had reached out and given their consent for Meg and Luke to legally adopt Tucker, Tilly and Tia.

Following his official retirement, Luke had made his dream of running a weekend rodeo camp for children a reality. After word got out that a famous retired bull rider ran the camp, kids came from all over the county with dreams of fame and fortune. The camp was currently booked for the next two years.

Meg was thrilled by the success of the destination wedding package offered at the B&B. Luke's idea to use the barn as a venue for ceremonies had been nothing short of genius. Of course, Meg had made sure she and Luke were the first to get married in the space. Now, each time they hosted a wedding, Meg had the opportunity to relive their own fairy tale–like day.

"Three babies! I sure hope at least one of them is a boy," Tucker called out from the other side of the fence.

Meg observed the triplets tending to the birch tree Luke had planted the day after they'd returned from their honeymoon. Her heart squeezed. Luke had explained to the children that the tree would provide year-round beauty that symbolized hope and new beginnings. Although the tree was for the entire family to enjoy, Meg knew the truth—Luke had planted it especially for Tucker. The two had a special bond.

"Come look!" Tucker motioned to the adults.

Luke opened the gate for Meg, wrapped his arm around her waist and joined the children next to the tree.

"What is it, son?" Luke placed his hand on Tucker's shoulder.

"There's three new branches sprouting from this limb." Tucker pointed to the largest branch on the birch.

"Just in time for your new brothers or sisters." Luke turned to Meg and smiled.

Tucker bounced on his toes. "This is so cool. I thought my family tree was broken." He looked up at Luke. "But thanks to you, it'll be stronger than ever." Tucker wrapped his arms tight around Luke's waist.

Meg watched her husband hug his son before he wiped the tears from his eyes. Happy tears where a smile always followed—that was what she prayed for her family. Warmth crept into Meg's heart. She finally had the home she'd always dreamed of. Her life was complete.

* * * * *

*If you enjoyed this emotional romance,
don't miss these other stories from
Jill Weatherholt:*

Second Chance Romance
A Father for Bella
A Mother for His Twins
A Home for Her Daughter
A Dream of Family

Available now from Love Inspired.

Find more great reads at www.LoveInspired.com.

Dear Reader,

Thank you again for spending time in Whispering Slopes. I hope you enjoyed reading the reunion story of Meg and Luke. Both struggled with emotional wounds from their past that prevented them from living the stable life God had planned for them.

Meg's desire for stability was a product of how she was raised, along with the guilt she carried over the death of her father. Luke struggled with having parents who loved him conditionally and, as a result, he equated winning accolades and money with stability.

During challenging times in our lives, we all have moments of feeling unstable. When it feels like our life is falling apart, we need to remind ourselves who is in charge. God never becomes unstable. He is the reason we can remain stable and at peace. When we look up to God to lead us, instead of ourselves, we find stability.

I love to connect with my readers. Please visit my website at jillweatherholt.com to sign up for my newsletter for the latest book news, giveaways and an inside peek at my writing life. Email me at authorjillweatherholt@gmail.com. I'd love to chat with you.

Jill Weatherholt

WE HOPE YOU ENJOYED
THIS BOOK FROM

LOVE INSPIRED
INSPIRATIONAL ROMANCE

Uplifting stories of faith, forgiveness and hope.

Fall in love with stories where faith helps
guide you through life's challenges, and discover
the promise of a new beginning.

6 NEW BOOKS AVAILABLE EVERY MONTH!

LIHALO2021

Get 4 FREE REWARDS!

We'll send you 2 FREE Books plus 2 FREE Mystery Gifts.

Love Inspired books feature uplifting stories where faith helps guide you through life's challenges and discover the promise of a new beginning.

FREE
Value Over
$20

YES! Please send me 2 FREE Love Inspired Romance novels and my 2 FREE mystery gifts (gifts are worth about $10 retail). After receiving them, if I don't wish to receive any more books, I can return the shipping statement marked "cancel." If I don't cancel, I will receive 6 brand-new novels every month and be billed just $5.24 each for the regular-print edition or $5.99 each for the larger-print edition in the U.S., or $5.74 each for the regular-print edition or $6.24 each for the larger-print edition in Canada. That's a savings of at least 13% off the cover price. It's quite a bargain! Shipping and handling is just 50¢ per book in the U.S. and $1.25 per book in Canada.* I understand that accepting the 2 free books and gifts places me under no obligation to buy anything. I can always return a shipment and cancel at any time. The free books and gifts are mine to keep no matter what I decide.

Choose one: ☐ **Love Inspired Romance**
              Regular-Print
              (105/305 IDN GNWC)

              ☐ **Love Inspired Romance**
              Larger-Print
              (122/322 IDN GNWC)

Name (please print)

Address   Apt. #

City   State/Province   Zip/Postal Code

Email: Please check this box ☐ if you would like to receive newsletters and promotional emails from Harlequin Enterprises ULC and its affiliates. You can unsubscribe anytime.

Mail to the Harlequin Reader Service:
IN U.S.A.: P.O. Box 1341, Buffalo, NY 14240-8531
IN CANADA: P.O. Box 603, Fort Erie, Ontario L2A 5X3

Want to try 2 free books from another series? Call 1-800-873-8635 or visit www.ReaderService.com.

*Terms and prices subject to change without notice. Prices do not include sales taxes, which will be charged (if applicable) based on your state or country of residence. Canadian residents will be charged applicable taxes. Offer not valid in Quebec. This offer is limited to one order per household. Books received may not be as shown. Not valid for current subscribers to Love Inspired Romance books. All orders subject to approval. Credit or debit balances in a customer's account(s) may be offset by any other outstanding balance owed by or to the customer. Please allow 4 to 6 weeks for delivery. Offer available while quantities last.

Your Privacy—Your information is being collected by Harlequin Enterprises ULC, operating as Harlequin Reader Service. For a complete summary of the information we collect, how we use this information and to whom it is disclosed, please visit our privacy notice located at corporate.harlequin.com/privacy-notice. From time to time we may also exchange your personal information with reputable third parties. If you wish to opt out of this sharing of your personal information, please visit readerservice.com/consumerschoice or call 1-800-873-8635. **Notice to California Residents**—Under California law, you have specific rights to control and access your data. For more information on these rights and how to exercise them, visit corporate.harlequin.com/california-privacy.

LIR21R2

COMING NEXT MONTH FROM
Love Inspired

THEIR SECRET COURTSHIP
by Emma Miller

Resisting pressure from her mother to marry, Bay Stutzman is determined to keep her life exactly as it is. Until Mennonite David Jansen accidentally runs her wagon off the road. Now Bay must decide whether sharing a life with David is worth leaving behind everything she's ever known...

CARING FOR HER AMISH FAMILY
The Amish of New Hope • by Carrie Lighte

Forced to move into a dilapidated old house when entrusted with caring for her *Englisch* nephew, Amish apron maker Anke Bachman must turn to newcomer Josiah Mast for help with repairs. Afraid of being judged by his new community, Josiah tries to distance himself from the pair but can't stop his feelings from blossoming...

FINDING HER WAY BACK
K-9 Companions • by Lisa Carter

After a tragic event leaves widower Detective Rob Melbourne injured and his little girl emotionally scarred, he enlists the services of therapy dog handler Juliet Newkirk and her dog, Moose. But will working with the woman he once loved prove to be a distraction for Rob...or the second chance his family needs?

THE REBEL'S RETURN
The Ranchers of Gabriel Bend • by Myra Johnson

When a family injury calls him home to Gabriel Bend, Samuel Navarro shocks everyone by arriving with a baby in tow. His childhood love, Joella James, reluctantly agrees to babysit his infant daughter. But can she forget their tangled past and discover a future with this newly devoted father?

AN ORPHAN'S HOPE
by Christina Miller

Twice left at the altar, preacher Jase Armstrong avoids commitment at all costs—until he inherits his cousin's three-day-old baby. Pushing him further out of his comfort zone is nurse Erin Tucker and her lessons on caring for an infant. But can Erin convince him he's worthy of being a father *and* a husband?

HER SMALL-TOWN REFUGE
by Jennifer Slattery

Seeking a fresh start, Stephanie Thornton and her daughter head to Sage Creek. But when the veterinary clinic where she works is robbed, all evidence points to Stephanie. Proving her innocence to her boss, Caden Stoughton, might lead to the new life she's been searching for...

LOOK FOR THESE AND OTHER LOVE INSPIRED BOOKS WHEREVER BOOKS ARE SOLD, INCLUDING MOST BOOKSTORES, SUPERMARKETS, DISCOUNT STORES AND DRUGSTORES.

LICNM0122A